NICK OF TIME

Fargo stepped into the firelit clearing, and the three kidnappers were surprised into silence. Susanna lay helpless against a tree.

"You owlhoots are at the end of your road," Fargo said, cocking his Colt and aiming it at them.

The skinny rat-faced one went for his gun. He was faster than a snake, but Fargo was faster. The bullet from Fargo's six-shooter cut through the man's heart, and he crumpled to the ground. The other two had their pistols out, firing wildly at him. Fargo stood his ground, methodically firing. The shirtless man was the next to die. Fargo's last bullet dropped the last man.

Only then did he notice the tiny stings on his arms and legs. Slugs had ripped through his shirt and pants, leaving shallow creases. He had come close to being gunned down. But the fight left those dead who deserved it. . . .

DENVER CITY GOLD

by

Jon Sharpe

A SIGNET BOOK

SIGNET
Published by New American Library, a division of
Penguin Putnam Inc., 375 Hudson Street,
New York, New York 10014, U.S.A.
Penguin Books Ltd, 27 Wrights Lane,
London W8 5TZ, England
Penguin Books Australia Ltd, Ringwood,
Victoria, Australia
Penguin Books Canada Ltd, 10 Alcorn Avenue,
Toronto, Ontario, Canada M4V 3B2
Penguin Books (N.Z.) Ltd, 182–190 Wairau Road,
Auckland 10, New Zealand

Penguin Books Ltd, Registered Offices:
Harmondsworth, Middlesex, England

First published by Signet, an imprint of New American Library,
a division of Penguin Putnam Inc.

First Printing, June 2001
10 9 8 7 6 5 4 3 2 1

The first chapter of this book previously appeared in *Flathead Fury*,
the two hundred thirty-fifth volume in this series.

Printed in the United States of America

The Trailsman

Beginnings . . . they bend the tree and they mark the man. Skye Fargo was born when he was eighteen. Terror was his midwife, vengeance his first cry. Killing spawned Skye Fargo, ruthless, cold-blooded murder. Out of the acrid smoke of gunpowder still hanging in the air, he rose, cried out a promise never forgotten.

The Trailsman they began to call him all across the West: searcher, scout, hunter, the man who could see where others only looked, his skills for hire but not his soul, the man who lived each day to the fullest, yet trailed each tomorrow. Skye Fargo, the Trailsman, the seeker who could take the wildness of a land and the wanting of a woman and make them his own.

Colorado Territory, 1859—
When greed sets off a gold-fever epidemic
and lead poisoning is a lethal symptom,
only the Trailsman can cure what ails.

1

The sharp crack of the bullwhip drowned out the buzz of the black flies bedeviling Skye Fargo. The Trailsman swatted at the annoying flies but knew it would do no good. Ever since the freight wagons had reached the uneven plains of eastern Colorado the flies had been swarming around his face, around his Ovaro, and around the long team of mules struggling to pull the heavily laden wagons bound for Denver City.

Fargo turned and scanned the terrain, hunting for level expanses to make the going easier for the freighters. Their mules were tuckered out from struggling over the gently rolling hills. Fargo had argued with Clem Parson before they left, but the wagonmaster had been adamant. He wanted Fargo to scout a shorter route and to hell with what that land west of Kansas City looked like. If they reached Denver City ahead of two competing freighters, Parson hoped to win lucrative contracts to supply the boomtown merchants with not only staple goods but the far more profitable luxury items.

In the back of the wagon Parson so expertly drove clanked and clattered a heavy iron Ramage press. The owner of the *Rocky Mountain News* had lost his printing press in a fire, and when Parson delivered this one, Bill Byers would again be able to put his newspaper into every eager Denverite's hand. Clem Parson figured the publicity gained would aid his cause since Byers was a generous man and helped anyone willing to see Denver City grow.

"There are gullies ahead," Fargo called to Parson. The grizzled mule skinner rocked back, ready to crack his whip again, but hearing Fargo's warning he relaxed and put the whip back into its holder at his side.

"Where do we head, then?"

Fargo knew how important it was to Parson to arrive before his competition, but bulling on and getting bogged down in the maze of ravines with such heavily laden wagons would slow them more than taking a rest.

"Stay here. I'll scout ahead and be back before sundown."

"Sundown? Hell, Fargo, that's two hours off!" Parson held up his hand to shield the sun and estimate how much travel time he would lose.

"Give the mules a rest now and you'll get twice the work out of them tomorrow," Fargo promised.

"I suppose," Parson said with ill grace. He stood in the driver's box and waved to the four wagons behind his to circle for the night.

"Don't worry so much, Clem. I'll get you to Denver within the week."

"Not if we spend all our time lollygaggin' around a campfire," groused Parson with mock vexation. "Do what you can, Fargo. You done all right up till now, so I don't reckon you'll abandon us out here on the plains."

"You can see the Rockies," Fargo said. "That's where we're heading. It's just a matter of finding the best route."

"Then get to it, man, get to it!" Parson grabbed his twenty-foot-long bullwhip and gave it a resounding crack in Fargo's direction. Fargo's Ovaro reared, pawed at the hot, still Colorado air, then took off at a trot in the direction of the troublesome ravines.

Fargo took every chance he could to ride along the top of the ridges crisscrossing the area so he could pick a path that would afford Parson and his wagons the easiest travel. After an hour of scouting, he thought he had found the best route—and one that would get the wagon train to Denver two days ahead of an already ambitious schedule. As he turned to retrace the route he had chosen, he reined back and stared at the bottom of a rocky-bottomed wash. He had been so intent on finding a route for the freighters he had missed a set of fresh tracks.

Fargo frowned, trying to figure out why anyone would follow the wash as the wagon obviously had. He dismounted and walked along the tracks. As he studied the ground more closely, the more curious he became. Not only had a wagon drawn by six oxen come along, so had no fewer than three horses, all shod. From the way the fitful wind had slightly rounded the wagon tracks but not the hoofprints, he guessed the riders were at least an hour behind the wagon.

In this empty land, he knew no reason riders would follow a wagon unless they were scouts returning to report on their survey. But three? More? What single wagon needed so many scouts?

Fargo found himself torn between returning directly to where Parson and his men camped and investigating this mystery. There was still an hour of sunlight left. If he galloped his sturdy pinto, the freighters might get another fifteen or twenty minutes of travel in today. Then he pushed that notion from his head. Parson would have already unhitched the teams and corralled the mules inside the ring of wagons. It would take more than fifteen minutes to get them hitched up again. Why risk traveling after sunset?

Not sure what worried him, Fargo mounted and rode along the trail left by the wagon. The wagon pulled out of the ravine and struggled across the prairie less than a mile from where Fargo had first come across the tracks. What puzzled him now was how the horses had vanished. Their riders had abandoned their pursuit of the wagon on some rocky ground.

Fargo knew he ought to turn around and report to Clem Parson. The freighter was a good employer, a generous man in spite of his gruffness, and was due a timely report on the result of Fargo's scouting. Parson deserved it, but something gnawed away at Fargo until he couldn't stand it any longer. He put his heels to the Ovaro's flanks and picked up the pace, chasing after the lone wagon.

As the red sun dipped behind the Rockies, showing the jagged peaks in the far distance clearly now, Fargo spotted the wagon. He reined back and watched as three dim figures bustled about the rear of the Conestoga. They weren't pitching camp. They were too engaged in pointing at the rear of the wagon and arguing with each other.

Fargo made no effort to hide his approach. He rode boldly and slowly so as not to spook the three. As he neared the wagon with its oxen team restlessly stirring in poorly maintained yokes, he saw two men in their twenties arguing while a woman somewhere between them in age stood by and stared at the wagon, as if this might miraculously fix it.

"Howdy," called Fargo, startling the trio. "See you've got a busted wheel. Anything I can do to help?"

"Who're you?" cried the younger of the men, reaching into the back of the wagon and pulling out a shotgun.

"Don't go pointing that at anyone you don't mean to shoot," Fargo said, irritated. "If you don't want my help, say so."

"I'm sorry, mister," the woman said, stepping out of the shadows that had partially hidden her face from Fargo's view. He caught his breath and knew why the man was so quick with the shotgun. If he had a woman as lovely as this one, he'd be protective of her, too.

The woman was small, hardly topping five feet, but her feminine figure was full and her face a vision of angelic loveliness. She brushed back a strand of dusty brown hair and looked at him with ginger-colored eyes that were both frank and inviting.

"We might need some help. Don't you agree, Zeb? Ben?"

Fargo saw the young man with the shotgun wince at the implied criticism of the armed greeting and pegged him to be Zeb. Ben was no more inclined toward friendliness than Zeb. Looking hard at them, Fargo thought they might be brothers.

"I'm Susanna Grafton," the woman said, coming over to him. He tipped his hat to her, then reached down and shook her hand when she thrust it out like a man might. As he introduced himself, he couldn't help noticing her shiny gold wedding ring as she impulsively brushed her hair away from her sparkling eyes.

Susanna stepped back and stared at the two men. Fargo wondered which of them was her husband and which was her brother-in-law. If he had to pick, the less impulsive Ben must be Mr. Grafton.

"Well, Mr. Grafton," Fargo said, dismounting, "let's see what the problem is."

"I can tell you," spoke up Zeb. "We busted the damned wheel!"

"Zeb! Watch your language!" snapped Susanna. This stopped Fargo in his tracks. She sounded more like a mother than an in-law—or a wife. Even a shrewish wife held her tongue in front of strangers.

"That's all right, ma'am," Fargo said. "Out here on the prairie, I've said worse things myself."

"He knows better," she said tartly. Then Susanna bit her lower lip and sucked in a deep breath when she realized the implied criticism of Fargo and his habits. "I apologize. I didn't mean it that way. It's just that we've had so much trouble getting this far."

"No need to apologize," Fargo said, meaning it. Seeing the rise and fall of her full breasts under the once-white but now dusty blouse was reward enough for him. He hadn't seen another human outside of Parson and his filthy freighters since they'd left Kansas City. Susanna Grafton was a vision of elegant femininity and even better than a long, cold beer for raising his spirits.

Fargo circled the two men, who warily watched him as if he would jump them at any instant. The left rear wagon wheel had lost two spokes.

"If you tried driving much farther like that, you'd break the wheel," he said.

"Can you fix it?"

"If you can get the wheel off and have a couple spare spokes, it won't take more than an hour." Fargo looked up into the twilight and saw the evening star winking down at him. He knew better than to make a wish on it. Susanna Grafton was already hitched, probably to Ben Grafton. That didn't dampen his desire to help them, though. Fargo saw they were rank greenhorns and needed to be shown how to do the most elementary repairs to their wagon.

"How'd you get this far without breaking a spoke or wheel?" he asked, grunting as he helped Zeb lever the wagon up so Ben could remove the wheel.

"We've been lucky," Zeb said. The young man carried a powerful lot of suspicion that Fargo had no desire to deal with at the moment. Ben dropped a couple new spokes to the ground by him, along with tools.

"Thanks," Fargo said dryly, and set to work getting the iron wheel rim off so he could replace the busted spokes.

"We . . . we can't pay you for your work," Susanna said anxiously, moving hesitantly toward him as if he were a raging fire and she was both cold and afraid of burning up.

"I'm not looking to get paid," Fargo said. "This is the neighborly thing to do. Where are you folks from?"

"St. Louis," Susanna said, ignoring both men's gestures to keep quiet. "We've been on the trail to Denver City for so long it seems like this is all we've ever known. It gets so lonely out here."

"At least you've got scouts to break the monotony," Fargo said, hammering the second spoke into place and fitting the iron rim back on.

"Scouts? I don't know what you mean. There's just us." Susanna said.

"Hush your mouth," snapped Ben. He took the shotgun from Zeb's hands and pointed it toward Fargo. "He's fixin' to rob us. That's why he's askin' all them questions."

"You want to lift the wagon so I can work the wheel back on or do you want to do it yourselves?" Fargo asked. He dusted off his hands, stared at Ben and the shotgun clutched in his shaking hands. "Good luck and good evening. Ma'am," Fargo said, touching the brim of his hat in Susanna's direction.

"Wait, don't be offended. Ben's just edgy. What men are you talking about?"

"I came on your tracks down in yonder wash. Following your trail, maybe an hour behind, were at least three riders. When you got out of the ravine, they set off for other parts."

"We don't know who they might be," Susanna said.

"He's lying," Zeb said. "He wants to spook us."

"This isn't St. Louis," Fargo said. "If I wanted to spook you, I'd mention that you're standing right next to a prairie rattler about ready to sink its fangs into your leg."

Zeb jumped a foot, wildly looking around. Fargo smiled without any humor at his small practical joke. They were all tenderfeet and had no business being on the trail alone.

"Maybe I'll see you in Denver," Fargo said, going to his Ovaro and getting ready to mount.

"Wait, Mr. Fargo, don't go like this. I am so sorry. I apologize for—"

"Don't do it, Susanna," snapped Ben. "Let him go."

"He helped us. We'd be stuck out here for days until you two figured how to fix that wheel. The least we can do is give him a decent meal."

Fargo's mouth began to water at the thought of something more than beans and salty buffalo jerky for dinner. Clem Parson had not hired on any muleteer worthy of being called a cook. Chuck with the freighters was always stomach-turningly similar to their prior meal, except when Fargo took time to hunt pheasant or rabbit along the way.

"Let him get on his way," chimed in Zeb. "We don't want to hold him up."

Fargo climbed into the saddle and stared down at Susanna Grafton. She was a lovely woman and angry at the way her husband and brother-in-law had treated him. Fargo knew better than to get involved in a family squabble. Whatever spooked the men was something they had to work out among themselves.

"Good evening," he said, turning to go. He halted,

then stood in the stirrups as he stared into the dying last rays of light sneaking between the sharp peaks of the distant Rocky Mountains.

"What is it, Mr. Fargo?"

"You say you didn't have anyone scouting for you?"

"Why, no, no one at all. We couldn't afford it."

"There are five men riding mighty fast in this direction." Fargo's mind raced. If the three he had followed had circled around to the west, they could have joined up with the other pair and waited for the Grafton wagon to rattle along. When it never appeared, the five men might have come looking for it. If so, Fargo knew their reasons for seeking out the Graftons weren't too peaceable or law-abiding.

"Robbers!" cried Zeb trying to grab the shotgun from Ben's hands.

"What do you think, Mr. Fargo?" asked Susanna. Her stricken expression would have held him here to defend the three greenhorns, even if his common decency had not been enough.

"I think he's right," Fargo said. "Can you hold them off?"

"Shoot them?" asked Zeb. "Yes!"

"Get to it," Fargo said. "If you have another gun, use it." His lake-blue eyes speared Ben Grafton.

"I don't know where it is," Ben stammered, flustered at the sudden turn of events.

"I do," Susanna said, pushing past him and rooting around in the wagon like a prairie dog digging its burrow. She came out with a small caliber Smith & Wesson.

"Wait until they get closer, then start firing," ordered Fargo.

"Where are you going?" asked Susanna, seeing him turn his horse.

"He's leaving us to be killed. He's a coward!" cried Ben.

Fargo wanted to hit the man for such an insult but had no time. If his hastily contrived plan was to work, he had to ride—fast. Leaving the three behind and letting them think he was a lily-livered coward rankled Fargo, but he knew staying to explain to them was not an option.

The first sharp crack of a gunshot echoed in the still evening air. From the sound. Fargo knew the approaching riders had opened fire. The report was nothing like what a shotgun or a revolver would make. He galloped until he got into a shallow ravine, cut north for a hundred yards, then urged the Ovaro up the steep cutbank and westward, setting up a one-man ambush from behind.

If he caught the outlaws, he might confuse them and make them think they had ridden into a trap where they were outnumbered and outgunned. Of course he would need the Graftons to open fire to pull it off.

Fargo cut another sharp corner and headed back south, hidden in the dust cloud kicked up by the five galloping outlaws. He barely made out their silhouettes as they shouted and fired wildly toward the wagon, not intending to hit any of the Graftons but wanting only to scare them into surrendering.

If the pilgrims did surrender, Fargo knew they were lost. They had to put up a fight or the road agents would have hostages Fargo could never free.

As he prepared to lose both the men and the lovely Susanna, he heard the sharp crack of a shotgun followed quickly by the duller "snap" of the six-shooter firing repeatedly. This was enough to force the road agents to slow their all-out attack and cluster together to rethink their assault. Fargo drew his Henry from its saddle sheath and levered in a round. He drew his Colt and used his knees to guide the Ovaro as it raced toward the outlaws.

Shouting like an attacking Cheyenne, Fargo began firing, the rifle in his left hand and the six-gun in his right. When the six-shooter came up empty he used both hands on the Henry for a more accurate shot. To his relief, he heard more shots fired from the direction of the Grafton wagon.

Fargo hoped the highwaymen would break off their attack and hightail it quick. His Colt was empty and his

Henry's magazine was getting perilously close to being exhausted. With only a round or two left in the rifle, Fargo saw the road agents make up their minds.

They ran like scalded dogs, leaving behind the wagon they had thought to be easy prey.

Slowing his headlong gallop, Fargo emerged from the dust cloud. He worried the Graftons would mistake him for one of the outlaws—or not care.

Ben jumped up, and took careful aim with his Smith and Wesson. Susanna cried out to stop, but Ben pulled the trigger. From a dozen yards away, Fargo heard the hammer fall on the empty cylinder. Never had a sound been so welcome.

Fargo rode more slowly, giving Susanna the chance to grab the pistol from her husband's grip.

"They're gone," Fargo said. "From the way they were riding, I don't think they'll be back any time soon."

"But you don't know?" Susanna asked anxiously.

"Ma'am, I can't rightly say. It's unusual seeing a gang attack a single wagon. They might go after a stage, but this is off the regular route into Denver City and frankly, there's not a whole lot you'd be carrying that would appeal to them." He eyed her significantly, letting Susanna finish his thought. Material goods like furniture and plow blades might not be what a road agent desired most, but a fine-looking doe like Susanna Grafton certainly was.

"Do you think they followed us?"

"From St. Louis?" Fargo scoffed at Zeb's notion they were that important. "I suspect the gang was riding along and saw easy pickings."

"We're not that easy to kill!" protested Ben. Susanna silenced him with a cold look.

"No, I can see that you're not," Fargo said, pouring a drop of oil on stormy water. He heaved a deep sigh and knew what he had to do with them. Leaving them to their own devices was a surefire way of getting them killed, even if they were only a few days' travel from Denver.

The alternative wouldn't satisfy anyone, but Fargo saw no way around it.

2

"We can get to Denver City from here," Ben Grafton said, thrusting out his chin belligerently.

"Thank Mr. Fargo for all he's done for us," said Susanna, elbowing him hard in the ribs. The man grunted and muttered something Fargo took to be the requested thank-you.

"I'm not leaving you alone out here," Fargo said. To him it was obvious the five road agents he had chased off might not have gone far. If they were hungry enough or the pickings had been slim, they might return to scout the solitary wagon. If the outlaws saw only the two men with Susanna, they would attack again. The outcome this time would be predictable.

Fargo had no hankering to dig three graves in this lonely, windswept land.

"We couldn't impose on you any more than we have already. You fixed our wheel—" Susanna began.

"Me and Zeb did most of the work," Ben said sullenly.

"And then you fought off those horrid robbers," Susanna finished, as if she had not heard her husband. Fargo shook his head in wonder. It hardly seemed possible they were married, but the wedding ring Susanna wore so prominently on her finger showed it was true. From the way they acted, Fargo had only to convince Susanna of the danger and she would impose her will on Ben and Zeb.

Somehow, that suited Fargo just fine.

"They're still prowling the countryside," Fargo said.

"If I go, they'll swoop down like vultures on you. How much ammo do you have left?" From the puzzled expressions on the two men's faces, Fargo knew the answer. "I'll see you to the wagon train I'm scouting for, then we can all go on into Denver."

"There's safety in numbers, Ben," Zeb said. The younger man fell silent when Ben glared at him.

"We're not backtrackin'," Ben said. "To go east when we're headin' west is all wrong."

"I have to talk to Clem Parson about you. His mules will pull faster than your oxen, in spite of his heavier load."

"Perhaps we can make it through the night without being attacked, Mr. Fargo. You can speak with this Clem Parson and then come back for us," Susanna said.

Fargo did not like the notion of leaving them alone, even for a few hours, but he had to do it if Ben Grafton refused to retrace his path for a few miles. He almost suggested that Susanna ride along with him, leaving the men behind, but that wouldn't have been proper.

"You hunker down and keep an eye out for those road agents," Fargo said. "I'll try to get back with Parson and the rest of the train by dawn." His mind raced as he estimated distances and travel times. Since he had not returned before sundown, Parson would be champing at the bit and wondering what had happened to him. News of almost helpless sodbusters needing help to get to Denver wouldn't set well with the cantankerous muleteer, but Fargo knew convincing Parson would take only a little work. Under the crusty exterior beat a heart of gold.

Fargo snorted. Some said it was fool's gold, but Fargo knew different.

"Hurry back," Susanna said, a plaintive note in her voice that made Fargo wonder what the situation in the Grafton party really was.

"Mrs. Grafton," he said, touching the brim of his hat politely, then turning his Ovaro and riding into the night. He heard Susanna start to say something but he was quickly swallowed by the night. Thin clouds moved restlessly across the sky, hiding the brilliant starlight that lit Fargo's path. It was a new moon, and he had to depend on the stars and his memory of the land to get back to Parson's camp. By riding through the ravines he had scouted ways around, Fargo spotted the dark outlines of the freight wagons a little before midnight.

Somehow, he was not surprised to see the coal on the tip of a cigarette burning some distance from the wagons. Fargo rode for it until Parson's rough features were distinct under the starlight.

"You surely did take your time gettin' back, Fargo," Parson said. He puffed a little harder until the coal blazed.

Fargo wasted no time on pleasantries and launched into a description of the trail the freighters had to follow—to join the Grafton party.

"Now why would I go out of the way to nursemaid these danged fools into Denver City?" Parson demanded. "There's big money restin' on me gettin' into town ahead of those other cutthroats. If I waste a day or two with settlers"—he spat the word as if it burned his tongue—"then I might not even be able to sell this load for more'n a bucket of horse piss."

"Traveling together benefits you both," Fargo said. "I chased off the outlaws. I don't believe I even winged one of those varmints."

"We got enough guns to fight 'em off without joinin' the settlers," Parson said.

"More wagons, less reward for attacking," Fargo pointed out. "It might benefit the Graftons more, but you'll have escorted a family to town willing to sing your praises."

"Don't need publicity like that," Parson said, but Fargo heard the freighter weakening.

"Imagine what an interview in Byers's paper will read like," Fargo pressed. "You get your name mentioned as being foursquare for new Denver City residents. Can't hurt, can it?"

"If it won't take longer than an hour or two, we can

drive over to see what they're willin' to say about me when we get to Denver," Parson said.

Fargo made certain the route was easy for the wagon train all the way to where he had left the Grafton family.

"You mean we got to eat their dust? This is worse than travelin' on our own," groused Zeb Grafton. He glared at the last freight wagon fifty feet ahead. Blankets of choking brown dust drifted back from Parson's slowly moving wagons, prompting the young man's complaint.

"Follow close and you'll be safe all the way into Denver," Fargo said.

Susanna Grafton stared up at him from beside the wagon. Again he was surprised at how tiny she was—and how womanly. Her ginger eyes danced as she stared at him. What Fargo read there wasn't proper for a married woman. Or was he misreading her? Fargo could not believe she was *that* grateful.

Or maybe he was guilty of wishful thinking. Susanna Grafton was one fine-looking woman.

"Only a day or two?" she asked.

"Clem is in a powerful hurry to reach town. He'd appreciate it if you could put in a good word for him, whenever you could."

"We don't owe him nuthin'," said Ben Grafton, poking his head out from the rear of the wagon. He jumped to the ground and came around.

"He's a good man. I have to ride ahead and scout for him."

"And look out for the road agents?" asked Susanna.

Fargo nodded curtly. He saw Ben was getting his feathers ruffled by the lengthy talk with his wife. Mounting his Ovaro, Fargo rode off fast, leaving the settlers to come to their own decision: Eat the muleteer's dust or hang back and provide easy prey for the robbers.

If Zeb or Ben had anything to say about it, the Grafton wagon might stay where it was until hell froze over. But Fargo doubted they had a single word to say about the decision. Susanna Grafton was the one in charge of their wagon.

Fargo roved a mile or two ahead of Parson, scouting the route into the Queen City of the Plains, as much out of duty to his employer as knowledge of the trouble he might get into if he stayed much longer around Susanna Grafton.

"Don't know how you done it, Fargo," Clem Parson said, scratching his stubbled chin. He held up a battered pocket watch on a gold chain and peered at the time, as if this meant anything. "You got us here three days sooner'n I'd've thought."

"That's five days ahead of the schedule you gave me when we left Kansas City," Fargo pointed out. "Moreover, you have a detailed map of the route I made, so you can follow the route again."

"Five days cut off the trip," cackled Parson. "I'll drive ole Costigan out of business, I will! Santiago won't have a chance, and no one else will even think of competing against me!"

"More power to you," Fargo said, thrusting out his hand. Parson shook it, his grip as powerful as Fargo's.

"You're a good man, Fargo. If I can do anything for you, you let me know. Anything at all."

"Well," Fargo said, grinning, "you can start by paying me."

"I ought to take out passage for your friends from your due," Parson said, returning to his usual outwardly grumbling mien. He dug around in his jacket until he fished out a small leather bag. He tossed it to Fargo.

"Thanks," Fargo said.

"You ain't gonna count it?"

"I trust you," Fargo said. "And if there's anything more you need from me, just ask."

"Get them settlers to Byers's *Rocky Mountain News* office and squawking 'bout how good a freighter I am," Parson said, jerking his thumb in the direction of the Grafton wagon.

Fargo laughed and parted company with Clem Parson, walking slowly toward the Grafton party. He had avoided them for the two days it had taken to reach

Denver City, but he had good reasons. Finding the smoothest trail to follow had been difficult until they were close to Denver. Then he had kept his distance to prevent any ill feelings with Ben Grafton.

Fargo had been on the frontier all his life and knew death as a constant companion. In all that time he had seen how a wrong, imagined or real, festered in some men until they couldn't live with it anymore. They eventually exploded by killing the object of their hatred. Fargo read men accurately and knew Ben Grafton to be one who would carry a grudge for a long time. Even worse, Fargo figured Ben to be the kind of man who would let a tiny affront trigger his outrage.

"Mr. Fargo!" cried Susanna, seeing him approach. "I worried you would go off and I wouldn't be able to thank you."

Fargo couldn't tell whether she was sweet on him or not, so he figured it was best to just do his job and not encourage her. "That's Denver," he said, ignoring her gratitude and pointing to the town on the far bank of Cherry Creek. "And that's Auraria." The two towns straddled the thin band of water meandering down from the Rockies, and had distinct personalities. Both vied for power and notoriety, but despite Auraria's larger population, Fargo put his money on Denver winning the struggle because of men like Bill Byers and General Palmer. They were huge supporters of anything in Denver, and Auraria lacked such unflagging promotion.

"They're lovely," Susanna said breathlessly. "But we won't be staying. We're moving on as soon as we can get more supplies."

"Where are you going? I thought you were settling here."

Susanna took his arm and steered him away from the wagon where Ben and Zeb struggled to get their gear unstowed so they could camp for the night. Twilight fell faster in Denver because of its nearness to the Front Range. The tall peaks shut off the sun earlier in the day than out on the prairie, and over in the foothills daylight was at least an hour less than here in town.

"No, we're pressing on . . ."

"You make it sound mighty secretive," Fargo said. He was self-conscious about the way Susanna held his arm. As they walked side by side, her hip bumped now and then into his, reminding him why he had been avoiding her in the first place. She was a married woman and even being alone with her like this wasn't right.

If her husband came after her, Ben Grafton might take it into his head to start shooting. It would be his right, but Fargo wasn't going to let any man gun him down. Better to avoid such unpleasantness by returning right away, rather than letting his lust for the lovely, petite woman get them all into a pickle.

"I want to share this with you. I know I can trust you," Susanna said.

"I'm not so sure of that, Mrs. Grafton," Fargo said in a low voice, increasingly uncomfortable with the situation. They had come down a gentle slope to the bank of the creek. The sun had dipped behind the mountains and stars twinkled in the black night sky, providing Fargo with the perfect backdrop to take advantage of the situation if he chose to do so.

Susanna looked at him strangely.

"I'm not so sure I can trust myself with you," Fargo continued, trying to explain.

"Don't concern yourself about that," Susanna said, turning and coming into the circle of Fargo's arms. He held her, a potent bundle of female passion. She looked up into his blue eyes, then stood on tiptoe and kissed him.

The kiss turned more passionate, and he found himself returning it in kind. They clung to one another, his strong arms around her waist and hers around his neck. Their lips crushed together until both gasped for breath.

Fargo broke off and tried to push her away.

"I can't. It's not right."

"What's not right?" Susanna asked.

"You're married."

For a moment, Fargo wondered what he had said that was so funny. Susanna clung to him and laughed so hard tears came to her eyes. She looked back up at him, kissed him fast, hard, with real lust.

"I'm not married," she said. "I wondered why you called me Mrs. Grafton."

"You're not Susanna Grafton?" Fargo's head spun in confusion now. Or was it only confusion? She was like locoweed, driving him out of his mind.

"Of course I'm Susanna Grafton, but I'm not married. You thought I was married to Ben or Zeb?" This set off a new bout of laughter.

"Ben," Fargo said. "He's not Ben Grafton?"

"Yes, he's Ben Grafton and I'm Susanna Grafton. But we're brother and sister. Zeb's my younger brother and Ben's three years older."

Fargo reached around and caught Susanna's slender wrist. He held her hand up so the starlight shone off the gold band on her left ring finger.

"How do you account for this?"

Susanna turned more somber, then said, "This was my mother's. I wear it so I'll never forget her. But I didn't think anyone would believe I was married, much less to my own brother!"

Fargo found everything he had to say all jumbled up. If he spoke now, it was sure to be wrong. He might never miss a trail, but he had misread Susanna, her brothers, everything about them.

He kissed her again, this time without the inhibitions of thinking she was a married woman. Susanna returned the kiss with growing desire, her tongue darting out to tangle with his before retreating. He felt her firm breasts pressing hotly into his chest and her body trembling in his arms like a race horse ready to run.

"Do you want this?" he asked, staring down into her bright eyes. He read the answer in her look before he heard her husky whisper.

"Yes," she said. Her hands began working at his gun belt, his pants, his buckskins. Before he knew it, he was naked from the waist down. Then Fargo felt the cool night breeze gusting past his hardening manhood as Susanna released it from its cloth prison.

He groaned softly as she took him into her mouth. The tongue that had rolled around his now tended him in more exciting ways. He put his hands on the back of the woman's head and guided her in the motion he enjoyed most. She eagerly gave him all the attention he wanted—for a spell. Then, as exciting as it was having Susanna minister to him like this, Fargo wanted more.

From the way her eyes blazed with craving for him, he knew she was ready for more, also.

Fargo sank to the ground and spread out his discarded clothes so Susanna could lie back. She purred like a kitten as he began unfastening the buttons on her blouse, touching the sleek, white skin revealed as he pulled back every layer. When her young, firm breasts popped from the frilly undergarments, Fargo knew he was lost.

He sank down and engulfed one taut nipple with his lips. Sucking hard, he pulled her up off the ground.

"Oh, Skye, you're amazing. You get me so excited!" She threw her arms around his head to hold him in place. His tongue laved her throbbing nipple, then slid down the sleek, steep cone of flesh to the deep canyon between her breasts. Fargo burrowed down to lick and lightly nip with his teeth. He was rewarded by Susanna's louder cries of joy.

Working his way up her other soft breast, he left behind a trail of dampness that cooled quickly in the evening breeze. With the creek burbling nearby and the wind blowing across their bodies, it was almost perfect for lovemaking.

Almost.

Fargo sucked hard on the cherry-red bud he found capping Susanna's left breast. When he pressed his tongue down hard, he felt her heart hammering away excitedly. The fire growing in his own loins told him it was time to make certain she was drawn as taut as a bowstring waiting to be plucked—only then would he let fly with his fleshy arrow.

Pushing her unwanted clothing out of the way, Fargo licked and kissed his way lower, across her slightly domed belly to the tangled, nut-colored bush hidden between her thighs. Turning first left and then right, he lavished kisses on the insides of her legs, his tongue becoming the key that opened her fully to him.

He touched the woman's nether lips and sent a ripple of desire rocking through her body.

"Yes, Skye, there, do it there. I'm burning up inside. Take me now!"

"Not yet," Fargo said. "I feel like playing some more!"

He thrust a finger inside and wiggled it around her heated interior. Susanna twisted and turned, groaning in her arousal. Her legs clamped back on him. Fargo kissed and licked at them again, causing them to spread wide once more. This time Susanna drew her knees up on either side of him, offering herself wantonly.

He continued running his finger in and out of her until her nectar began coating his hand. She was ready for him—and there was no question he was ready for her. Fargo moved back up her body, kissing as he went. Susanna grabbed for him, her fingers locked behind his head to pull his face down to hers.

Again they kissed hard. This time a new element was added. Fargo scooted forward until the tip of his fleshy column bumped into Susanna's nether lips. They both gasped when Fargo positioned himself properly and buried the knobby end of his stalk within her trembling body.

"Yes, Skye, do it. Do it!" she cried.

Susanna was thrust past coherent speech. Fargo's hips took on a life of their own and slammed forward. He buried himself fully in her, then he paused to revel in the tightness, the heat, the feel of an aroused woman responding fully to his manhood. When he feared he would lose control like a young buck, he pulled back.

"Oh, no, no," moaned Susanna. "You're so big in me. Again. Again!"

He obeyed his own instincts—and her fervent command. Slipping smoothly back into the sheath of female flesh, he rotated his hips this time as if he were a spoon in a mixing bowl. When he was at the brink of losing control, Fargo pulled back. Then he began ramming her harder and faster. He found himself melting together with the woman as they wrestled together passionately on the bank of the creek. Faster and faster moved his hips until every powerful thrust completely lifted her off the ground.

Fargo was never quite sure when he lost control. The rising tide of white-hot lust spilled itself as Susanna cried out in release. He felt her body clamp down hard all around his hidden length, as if she had found a delightful way of milking him. They rolled over and over on the ground, locked together in mutual yearning. Panting and sweaty, they lay in each other's arms.

"We need to wash off some of the mud," Fargo said, pushing away from the naked woman under him.

"We did roll around a bit in the dirt. I needed a bath, anyway." She grinned as she boldly stared at him. "I'll wash your back if you'll wash mine."

Fargo glanced at the creek, then returned her smile. "I need more than my back washed."

"So do I!"

Laughing like children, they splashed into the water and rinsed off the dirt and sweat until they were ready to take each other on again.

3

Fargo lay with his arm encircling Susanna's naked shoulders. She was half turned toward him, her warm breast pressed intimately against his chest. He felt her soft, feathery breath on his flesh and knew she was working up to telling him something he probably did not want to hear.

"Skye?"

"Do you think we should get back to the wagon?" He worried that her brothers might take it into their heads to do something reckless. The way they waved their shotguns and six-shooters around told him they couldn't hit the broad side of a barn if they were locked inside it. What worried him was the pair starting to spray lead and hitting someone by accident.

Like him.

"No, not yet," she said. Susanna scooted around and propped herself up on one elbow so she could look him squarely in the eye. In the dim light her brown eyes took on a golden tint.

"I'm moving on, now that I've mapped the route for Parson," he said. Fargo had no clear idea where he was headed, but it was somewhere far away from Denver. Men like Parson fed the beast and made Denver City grow like a catamount cub in a high mountain meadow. Fargo didn't hold that against the freighter, but he didn't have to like the rapid growth and the incredible rush of men—and women—to the area. Eventually they would build a city so large he would hardly be able to stand it.

When that happened they would start spilling out into the Front Range, into the land Fargo thought of as his own.

"That's good to hear," she said. "I had hoped you weren't staying in Denver to, uh, partake of the pleasures here."

"I've found some mighty fine pleasure already," he said, running the tip of his finger across her nipple. Susanna giggled and then swatted his hand away.

"So have I, but I'm not staying here, either," she said. Her face took on a glow Fargo had seen before, usually in men about ready to tell him how they were going to strike it rich. "In St. Louis I bought a map."

"A treasure map?" he asked. Fargo sank back and stared up at the stars. He had heard of unscrupulous men who sold fake treasure maps to greenhorns like Susanna and her brothers. "What is it? Spanish treasure left by the conquistadors? Metal stolen by Indians and hidden, since they don't care for gold?"

"No, silly," Susanna said. "Nothing like that. We wouldn't know how to go about finding treasure. This is something better."

"Better?" Fargo sucked in his breath. Before Susanna spoke, he knew what she was going to say.

"A map showing the next big gold strike in the Front Range. We're going to be fabulously rich. All we have to do is get there, stake a claim, and pull the gold from the stream by the handful!"

"Why would anyone sell you such a valuable map?" Fargo asked.

"It was such a sad story. This old man's son had found the gold and made the map. He was killed. When his belongings were sent along to the old man, the map was there."

"And the old man could never survive the trip, so he sold it to you and your brothers."

"Why, yes, that's right! He was dying himself and wanted a few dollars to ease his decline."

"How few? What did you pay him?"

"Around five hundred dollars. It was all we had in

cash, but he took it. He was such a nice old man. We had to sell our parents' house and belongings to get the wagon and team to come out here."

Fargo said nothing. The "nice old man" had probably sold the map a dozen times to suckers like Susanna. Chances were good he had never had a son, or if he had, it was one that never strayed to this side of the Mississippi River. Con men and hustlers were always on the lookout for the gullible and the greedy. Fargo felt a pang that Susanna happened to be a little bit of both.

"We have a map, but getting lost on the prairie showed us how much we need a man like you to guide us to . . ." Susanna's voice trailed off. She said almost contritely, "I'm sorry. I won't burden you with the name of the town unless you hire on."

"The town?" This piqued his curiosity. "He sold you a map to a town in the Front Range?"

"Well, yes. But the instructions are to a specific spot on the river near the town."

This was a twist to an old scheme that made Fargo wonder. Swindlers were seldom too specific, hinting at pots of gold at the end of a rainbow rather than naming a town.

"An actual town? You checked?"

"Of course I did. I'm not stupid, Skye. Nugget exists!"

He heard her gasp when she realized she had named the town. Fargo had never heard of Nugget but that did not surprise him. Boomtowns were known to sprout like toadstools after a spring rain and then die just as fast.

"You're sure this place is real?" he asked, skepticism in his voice.

"It must be. Promise you won't tell Ben or Zeb I said anything. They don't trust you. I can trust you, can't I?" Her fingers lightly danced across his chest and moved lower.

Fargo wondered if others from St. Louis who had been sold the bogus gold map had shown up in Nugget. They all might converge on the same claim, meaning the swindler knew something about the lay of the land. He might even have a partner in Nugget looking to further rob the eager treasure seekers. It was a long shot, but Fargo thought it might be possible for him to get Susanna's money back. He owed her nothing, but he never liked seeing anyone flimflammed out of so much money. What made it worse in this case was that Susanna and her brothers had sold off everything in St. Louis left to them by their parents and then trooped halfway across the country to claim their due.

"I wasn't heading in any particular direction. The Front Range is as good as anywhere else."

"Then you'll do it! Oh, thank you, Skye!" She proceeded to show him how grateful she was, leaving him exhausted and aching.

"If I charged you a hundred dollars, would that make you feel any better?" Fargo asked Ben Grafton. The young man glared at him, then turned hot eyes toward his sister.

"You shouldn't have told him everything," Ben accused.

"I don't want to be a goldminer," Fargo said honestly. He knew what backbreaking work it was, whether burrowing like a mole into hard rock or panning all day or using a rocker on a stream. A big strike brought only a few ounces of color for every ton of dross. Fargo preferred spending a day stalking a deer that would feed him for a week or prowling the high country and bagging an elk, whose meat might be traded for supplies that could last him throughout an entire winter.

"You'll let us do the work, then rob us," Zeb piped up. Both Susanna and Ben glared at him until he subsided.

"We need Mr. Fargo to guide us. Remember what happened out on the prairie? He can help us get to Nugget. And I haven't told him anything more than that," Susanna said guiltily.

Ben turned sullen, then shrugged. "Do what you want. I reckon it's all right for you to show us the way."

"You'll be looking at my back the whole way," Fargo promised, knowing he was the one taking the risk.

"Bet that's not what Sis has been lookin' at," muttered Zeb. The younger man turned red with embarrassment and then hurried off to get the oxen hitched.

"Here's the map showing the location of Nugget," Susanna said, holding out a crumpled piece of paper for Fargo's examination. She kept the map folded so written instructions on the bottom were hidden. He figured this was the description of the actual gold strike. Whether or not Susanna completely trusted him or just hid the map's details to appease her brothers did not matter to Fargo. He found a few road marks and determined that Nugget was in the Rockies, a short distance southwest of Denver City. Once he got closer, he would scout around and find it. Until then all he had to do was follow well established roads.

"Everybody got rich back in '49," Zeb said, returning from hitching up the team. "They all struck out for California and came back so loaded down with gold, they could hardly walk. We're not passin' up the chance for that now."

Fargo wondered if the young man believed that. As far as he had ever heard, most of the Forty-niners flocking to California had ended up poor as a church mouse, like Sutter—the man who had started it all. The only fortunes made were by those supplying the prospectors with their equipment and food.

He had no doubt the current gold rush with Denver at its heart would play out the same way. People like Susanna and her brothers would toil endlessly for nothing while storekeepers—and men like Clem Parson—made a decent living off them.

"Ready, Fargo?" demanded Ben Grafton as he climbed into the driver's box beside Susanna. Zeb had already jumped into the rear of the wagon and sat with his bandy legs swinging.

"Let's go find some gold," Fargo said, climbing in the saddle and heading his Ovaro toward the towering purple peaks of the Front Range.

* * *

By the time Ben maneuvered the wagon up the narrow, deeply rutted road toward the sign proclaiming the entrance to Nugget, he was almost cordial toward Fargo.

"There it is. You done it, Fargo, you brought us here double-time. I didn't think you'd do it, but you did. Not a single wrong turn anywhere."

"When can we get to pannin' for the gold, Ben?" asked Zeb from the rear of the wagon.

"We need to find the location on the map," Susanna said, as eager as her brothers.

Fargo pushed his hat back and studied the sign. It was freshly painted and done in neat lettering, unlike most boomtowns. The road from the foothills into Nugget was also well tended, but this wasn't too hard to explain. New towns often went out of their way to be sure newcomers had no trouble arriving.

Fargo rode ahead of the Grafton wagon, taking in the sights. That there was only one saloon told him there weren't more than a hundred miners out in the hills surrounding Nugget. A single general store stood next to it and beyond that was the assay and land office. On the other side of the main street stood a small jailhouse. Next to it was a doctor's surgery. A half dozen other stores stretched along either side of the road. Nugget had not grown so large that it needed a second street. Yet.

"How do we find this spot?" asked Zeb, peering over his sister's shoulder. Susanna pushed back her unruly hair as she spread the map out on her skirts, trying to make sense of it.

"You want me to find the spot?" Fargo asked.

"We can do it. We got this far," Ben said, his mood turning frigid toward Fargo again.

"Your call," Fargo said. "Go stake your claim. I'll hang around Nugget for a spell."

"You won't go until I can, uh, I mean, we can see you again?" Susanna's ginger eyes went wide with dismay that he might leave without spending more time with her. That was the furthest thing from Fargo's mind.

"I'll be here. Go find your destiny." He cocked his head to one side and pointed upslope into the hills. "I hear a stream in that direction. You might see if that's where your map takes you."

"Lookee, Ben, it does. See," said Zeb, his finger stabbing down. "Turn the map around this way and that's the spot!"

Ben glared at Fargo, then snapped the reins and got his oxen moving slowly through town. Fargo dismounted and waited to see what would happen when the Graftons passed through. A well-dressed man emerged from the land office, thumbs hooked into his vest as he watched the Graftons on their way from town. A smile curled his lips and caused his handlebar mustache to twitch. Whoever he was, the man was important in these parts. Fargo had seen his like a hundred times over.

Who better to ask about Nugget?

Fargo hitched his Ovaro to a post and went across the street. The man saw him coming and smiled even more broadly.

"Welcome, stranger. You just come into Nugget?"

"That I did," Fargo answered. "I need some information."

"You've come to the right person. My name's Harry Austin, and this is my town."

"You've got quite a place to be proud of," Fargo said, buttering Austin up. The man glowed with praise.

"You look like a mountain man rather than a prospector. You interested in doing some hunting to supply meat for the general store?"

"Yours?"

"Naturally."

"I might be willing," Fargo allowed.

"Then let's go have a drink to seal the deal at the Lucky Nugget," Austin said.

"The saloon's yours, too?"

"What else?"

Together Fargo and Austin entered the saloon. The few men in the place this early in the afternoon turned and looked at Austin. Fargo had the feeling they worked for the man and were a bit worried at being caught drinking on his time, but they relaxed when they saw Fargo and went back to their beers.

"What'll it be, mister?" Austin asked.

"The name's Fargo and a shot of Billy Sullivan's finest would be nice."

"Get that new bottle of rye," Austin told the barkeep. The small, mousy man's head bobbed as if it was on a spring. He dived under the bar and came up with a bottle of the rye whiskey that Fargo thought was legitimate. Most saloons bought one bottle, the owner drank the contents and then refilled the bottle with his own tarantula juice to dupe the patrons.

"You've got good taste in liquor, Mr. Fargo. Here you are." Austin poured from the newly opened bottle. Fargo sampled it, then let the liquor slide down his throat and settle warmly in his belly.

"Topnotch," Fargo said, savoring the flavor.

"Glad you like it." Austin sampled his whiskey again, then put the mostly full shot glass on the bar. "You came into town with those folks in the wagon. You with them?"

"We rode along the trail into Nugget," Fargo said, skirting the truth. "They told me they'd bought some property along a river. They intend to pan for gold there."

"Well, well," said Austin, shaking his head. "I hate to disillusion those fine people, but they never purchased the mineral rights on any land. Hell, they haven't even claimed the land."

"They had a map," Fargo said.

"Ah, yes, one of those floating around back East. We're getting more and more pilgrims coming out here with those maps. I don't rightly know who's responsible, but a map is all it is. There's no land that goes with it. I hope your friends didn't pay too much for the map."

"I can't say," Fargo said, dodging the matter of his relationship with the Graftons. He was aware of Harry Austin studying him closely. Any poker player worth his weight eyed his rivals looking for hints of the cards held close to the chest.

"Nugget is a growing town and needs all manner of folks to help it grow even bigger."

"Is the hunting good in the hills?" asked Fargo.

"It was better before the town was established about six months back. The deer are moving into higher meadows as the traffic along the road from Denver City increases and miners go out to shoot themselves some dinner."

"Why do you need a hunter, then?"

"Truth to tell, most of the prospectors are piss-poor hunters. I can convince them to buy my meat so they can save their time for hunting gold."

"You can take their money, too," Fargo said, sipping at a second shot of whiskey. Austin still had to finish his first. He either was not much of a drinker or he intended to get Fargo drunk. The whiskey went down so smooth and easy Fargo almost considered seeing how far Austin would go paying for the liquor.

Harry Austin laughed heartily. "I can see I'm not putting anything over on you. Of course I'll take their money. That's my business. The men I have working for me, like Whip Ballinger over there, lack any real skill hunting."

"Looks like everything in Nugget is your business." Fargo glanced at the whipcord-muscled man with an ugly hatchet-thin face seated at the far table and noted his cold look. If he had ever seen a gunfighter, this man was it. Fargo saw Austin turn wary as he realized Fargo had pegged Ballinger's occupation perfectly.

"I never was much for prospecting. My father tried it, to no avail. I decided I enjoyed the thrill of the chase but not the heartbreak after a day of futile hunting. So I sell to the brave lads willing to sally forth and risk their lives to find a fortune."

It was a fine speech. Fargo reckoned Austin had given it word for word more than once.

"Pretty soon they'll be building a statue to you in the town square, when the town has a square," Fargo said.

Austin fixed a gimlet eye on him, wondering if Fargo was needling him or stating a simple opinion.

"The real heroes are those who toil daily at the small jobs." Austin turned and said to the barkeep, "You keep this gentleman's glass filled, you hear? I've got work to do at the bank."

"Thanks for your hospitality," Fargo said, knowing he would sample a little more of the whiskey—but not too much. The potent whiskey was already going to work on him. He did not think Nugget was the kind of place where he should lose even a bit of common sense or sharp wit.

Harry Austin spoke at length with Whip Ballinger, then left, whistling a jaunty tune and looking on top of the world. Fargo waited until he had gone before questioning the bartender about Nugget—and its founder.

"I didn't see a bank. Is Austin putting one in?"

"Surely is, but he's having trouble getting a safe up from Denver, so he does most business out of the general store," the barkeep said, licking his lips as he stared at the rye whiskey Fargo had in his shot glass. The man eagerly took the glass when Fargo shoved it across to him and silently bade him to share the bounty.

"What else does Mr. Austin own in Nugget?"

"Everything. Every damned thing, including me," the barkeep said with some bitterness. "I ran up too much debt with him over at the general store. I'm here working it off and will be for another year."

"What about the others?" Fargo indicated the men whispering to each other at a table across the Lucky Nugget. The barkeep did not have to answer. They were beholden to Austin, also, and probably for the same reason.

The town was being run with an iron hand, and that hand had just offered Fargo a drink and a job. He wondered what this meant for the Graftons and their quest for gold. He thought a spell, then decided they would never find out what it meant to be in debt to Harry Austin. When they discovered they had bought a worthless map, they would return to Denver and possibly even St. Louis, sadder, wiser, and a sight poorer.

Fargo sat at a table near the door and savored the

liquor for another hour until he heard a furor outside. He turned his chair slightly and made sure his Colt was near to hand. He straightened when a sweaty, filthy Ben Grafton shoved through the doors and looked around, a wild look in his eye.

"What is it?" Fargo asked, getting the man's attention. Ben pulled up a chair, sitting close to Fargo.

"We found the spot on the river," Ben said, out of breath as if he had run miles. "We found it and—"

"And you worked it all afternoon," Fargo said.

"Yes, we did. Zeb and me. We worked it and—"

"And you didn't find anything."

Ben's eyes went wide, and he shook his head. "No, Fargo, we found gold! Tons of it! And it's all ours!"

4

"It's fool's gold," Fargo said flatly. Everything he had decided was true would be turned upside down if Ben Grafton was right about finding real color in the stream. The notion that Susanna and her brothers had bought a bona fide map showing the location of a gold strike was too incredible to believe.

"Here, look at it. Tell me. Do you think it's fool's gold?" Ben reached into his pocket and pulled out a nugget slightly larger than a pea. Fargo snatched it from his grip when he saw others in the saloon paying closer attention. In spite of Ben whispering the news, he had alerted them that gold was near. Fargo did not want to advertise a real strike until he made sure of its authenticity.

"Let's go outside," Fargo said. He felt buoyed by drinking Austin's whiskey and ready to whip his weight in wildcats. He stepped into the bright Colorado sun and held up the nugget. Fargo swallowed hard when he saw how much gold was in the small rock. If they found more rock with this percentage of gold, it would assay out to several ounces a ton and make the Graftons wildly rich.

"There's more in the river," Ben said, taking the nugget back from Fargo. "You're the expert. Is it real?"

"It looks like the real thing to me, but you should have it assayed, just to be sure," Fargo said. He pointed to the assay office across the street.

"Why not? We own the claim." Ben Grafton strutted across the dusty street, cock of the walk now that he had a fortune in gold waiting for him. Fargo followed the man into the assay office.

The chemist looked up from a month-old copy of Byers's *Rocky Mountain News,* clearly bored with life.

"What can I do for you gents?" he asked, climbing to his feet as if every joint in his body ached.

"I need to know how much gold's in this," Ben said, dropping the nugget on the desk. The chemist sniffed contemptuously, as if everything he saw was worthless. Fargo watched as the man's eyes widened. He snatched the nugget up and held it high so it caught a ray of light coming through a western window.

"Where'd you find this?" demanded the assayer.

"What's it worth?" countered Ben.

"Let's take a look and see."

Fargo watched as the chemist worked on the nugget with aqua regia and beakers of other strange concoctions until he pushed back his sleeves and heaved a deep breath.

"You got a winner here, boy," the chemist said. "I'll give you twenty dollars for this rock."

"Why not?" Ben said. "There's plenty more where that came from."

"Where might that be?" asked the chemist, a mite too eager for Fargo's liking.

"What's all the fuss?" asked Harry Austin, strutting into the assay office. He stopped behind them, his thumbs hooked in the armholes of his vest, his belly protruding.

"I bought a map. I own the claim. I mean we do, my brother'n me. And my sister's there, too, so don't think of jumpin' our claim!"

"Claim? What claim might this be? Not that it matters one whit. Truth is, you don't own anything around here. I do. I own just about everything, except the parcels I've sold to some miners who showed up a few weeks back."

"Here," Fargo said, pointing out on a wall-mounted map the stretch of river where the Graftons had found the nugget. "Is this all yours?"

"Surely is," Austin said with some relish. "I can prove

it, too. Check the land deeds." He pointed to a thick book at the far end of the counter. Fargo didn't have to look to know the answer. Austin had the entire area under this thumb.

"But we—" began Ben.

"What is the land worth to you?" asked Fargo, his mind racing. Austin might not have heard the chemist's offer for the nugget.

"Well, now if you found yourself some gold there, that increases the value. I don't reckon I could let it go for anything less than five hundred dollars."

Fargo blinked. This was a ridiculously low price considering the value of the nugget Ben had presented for assay.

"We'll buy it!" blurted Ben before Fargo could caution him to silence. Something was wrong with Austin's easy acceptance of a sale for a price that was high but not exorbitant.

"Sold," Austin said, thrusting out his hand. The two men shook. "Now, you willing to pay in scrip or do you have some hard currency? Like gold dust? I'll give you a five percent discount if you pay in specie. I don't cotton much to those Denver banks and their paper money."

Ben licked his lips and shifted his weight from foot to foot. Fargo knew the Graftons were tapped out after buying the map and buying the gear required to make the trip from St. Louis.

"I . . . I can get it," Ben said lamely.

"It happens you are in luck, old son," Austin said cheerfully. "I'm getting my bank up and running and I am in sore need of customers."

"Customers?" Ben asked dully. "I can't put any money into your bank."

"Banks *loan* money. I'd be more than happy to loan the money for you to purchase this plot of land," Austin said. "Thirty percent will be what we will usually charge, but twenty-five percent interest seems a fair rate for a new bank, a prized customer newly come to Nugget, and—" Austin cut off his speech when he saw Fargo's cold gaze. Austin grinned, as if challenging Fargo.

"I'll take it. We're hard workers. We can pay it back in nothing flat," Ben said.

"You are a lucky man, yes, sir," said Austin, reaching into his pocket. "I just happen to have a loan application with me. Sign here and here."

Everything was moving way too fast. Fargo tried to speak up, but Ben silenced him with an icy gaze as he reached out and signed the papers. Greed had reared its ugly head, and Fargo could do nothing to keep it from driving the Graftons into trouble.

Fargo had seen enough men hustled out of their grubstakes to know Harry Austin was a con man. His entry into the assay office had been at precisely the right instant to make it seem as if he didn't know the value of the land he was selling. The price was low for prime gold-bearing land, but the interest on the loan amounted to usury. He had set the price high but not so high he scared off Ben Grafton.

"Very good. I'll record the deed in a while in that very book," Austin said, pointing again at the ledger on the counter. "Do you need any supplies? The general store is willing to let you run a tab."

"I—later," Ben said, looking at Fargo again. The young man's eyes glowed with an almost fanatical light. He had gold fever. Bad. "I need to go tell my brother and sister what's happened."

"The nugget," called out the chemist. "What about it?"

"I'll keep it, for the moment. A souvenir of the biggest strike along the entire Front Range!" Ben went outside and whooped.

"Are you going to work for him or have you decided to take my offer of employment?" Harry Austin asked Fargo. The man's mustache twitched with merriment, and Fargo knew he was being mocked.

"I'm still thinking on it. Thanks for the whiskey."

"Any time, Mr. Fargo. If you get tired of panning for gold, the offer will still be open." Whistling, Austin left the assay office. Fargo glanced at the chemist, who had already gone back to his newspaper as if he hadn't seen the goldangedest, biggest, finest nugget ever. Fargo found Ben outside, hugging himself and laughing.

"We done it, Fargo, we done it! We struck it rich!"

"That's a powerful big claim to make after you found one nugget," Fargo said.

"It's a big claim, all right. And we own it! We'll haul out the gold by the ton!"

"You mind if I look over your claim?" Fargo saw Ben turn wary. He had come into Nugget bubbling over with the news. He had to tell someone, and he knew Fargo. Now that the news was out and the land belonged to the Graftons, he returned to his suspicious ways.

"I reckon we owe it to you," Ben said reluctantly. "But it's ours. We bought the map, and I signed for the land."

"It's all yours, all right," Fargo said, a dry note to his voice.

Harry Austin watched them as they left Nugget, smiling and waving as they passed the bank.

"Isn't it wonderful, Skye?" Susanna cried, clapping her hands together and bouncing up and down. "We're rich!"

Fargo saw both brothers stop and glare at him. He read their expressions. *They* were rich, not Fargo. This was *their* claim, not his. And from the way Ben looked from Fargo to Susanna and back, the gold was not all the Grafton brothers considered off limits.

"Have you pulled any more gold out of that stream?" Fargo asked. The brothers had used pans to work a small section of the stream. Finding the first nugget had been a stroke of luck—and Fargo was not inclined to believe in luck over hard work.

"We have, Skye," Susanna said, still excited. She grabbed his arm and steered him toward the edge of the stream. Fargo could hardly believe his eyes at the small pile of nuggets there. None was as large as the one Ben had brought to town, but there were several hundred dollars' worth of gold.

"We got this, too," Zeb said, ignoring his brother's

gesture to keep silent. The younger Grafton pulled out a small leather bag and spilled a few grains of gold dust into the palm of his hand.

"How much do you think it's worth, Skye?" Susanna moved closer. He felt the heat from her body pressed into his and her excitement at the find.

"I'm no expert, but you might have several hundred dollars there," Fargo said. "Almost enough to pay off the loan and the bank."

"We can get more real quick, Mr. Fargo," said Zeb. "The whole danged creek's bustin' at the seams with gold!"

"You look upset, Skye. What's wrong?"

Fargo led the woman away from where her brothers returned to their avid panning before saying what was on his mind.

"Why would Austin sell land with this much gold on it?"

"Why, he didn't know. That's obvious. The man we bought the map from said his son had been most secretive."

"Austin owns all this land. Other miners have come here hunting for gold. Why did they miss a strike this rich?"

"They weren't as good as Ben and Zeb," Susanna said in vexation. "What are you getting at?"

"It's a mighty big coincidence that Austin wasn't aware of the gold in the only river in the region. He's been here long enough to put up a town."

"That might be why he didn't know what was really here," Susanna said. "He was too busy building the saloon and store and all the rest."

Fargo saw he couldn't argue with the woman. The glint of gold had mesmerized her and her brothers into thinking they were smarter than a sharper like Harry Austin.

"You're jealous, that's all," Susanna said, with a steel edge to her words.

"I'm happy for you and wish you only the best," Fargo said. "It's about time for me to get on back to Denver City."

"But I—but, Skye, it's almost dark. You ought to stay here. For the night," she said almost lamely. Her fingers roved up and down his arms, moving to his chest. He backed off before those questing fingers found the spot that would weaken his resolve and make him stay.

"Good-bye, Susanna. I meant it when I said I want only the best for you and your brothers."

"Good-bye, Skye," she said, coming up on tiptoe to brush her lips lightly across his. Then Susanna dashed back to the river, holding her skirts up so they wouldn't drag the ground. She dropped beside Zeb and the two of them poked through a new pan filled with sand and water, hunting for the bright specks that would make them rich.

Fargo found himself wanting to stay but convinced himself it wasn't a smart thing to do. The Grafton brothers were suspicious of him. When it came to their gold, they were needlessly jealous. Fargo knew he would have enjoyed sharing their sister's bed again, and for that reason he had to leave Nugget. Gold and women were a dangerous mix.

He cut across the countryside so he wouldn't have to ride back down Nugget's main street. Fargo had no reason other than a vague feeling he was buying the Graftons time if Harry Austin did not find out right away that he had left. The Grafton family was ripe for the picking, if Austin had his sights set on them. What the plan might be, Fargo was at a loss to determine, since so much gold had been pulled out of the stream already.

Then he shrugged it off. He wished Ben, Zeb, and Susanna nothing but good luck and hoped they became the wealthiest residents of Colorado. Gold panning was not for him, nor was hunting meat for the likes of Harry Austin.

As Fargo came out onto the road leading back to Denver, he heard the loud neighing of a horse followed by a single gunshot. He eased the Colt from his holster to be sure it was ready for action, then urged the Ovaro down the dusty road.

As he rounded a bend, he saw a man laying facedown in the weeds. Fargo reined back and drew his six-shooter. Every sense came alive as he listened and watched and sniffed the air for danger. All he caught was the faint acrid whiff of gunsmoke. He dismounted and approached the fallen man.

Whatever danger the fallen man possessed spilled away in a crimson pool. Fargo saw a tiny hole in the back of the man's head. As he turned him over a larger bloody hole in his forehead showed the man had died instantly from the bushwhacker's brutal, cowardly attack. One pants pocket had been ripped away, hinting that a wad of greenbacks might have been stolen. If so, the killer had known where his victim carried his money. None of the man's other pockets had been turned out in a hunt for other wealth.

Fargo sniffed the air like a wolf, turning to look uphill. The scent of saddle leather and stale sweat led him a few paces until he saw the tracks of two horses going upslope. One carried a rider. The other did not.

"A backshooter and a horse thief," Fargo said with distaste. He whistled and his Ovaro trotted to him. Fargo mounted and followed the hoofprints to the top of the hill. From here, the trail led deeper into the mountains over rocky ground.

Fargo picked up the pace. The killer shouldn't be more than a few minutes ahead of him not knowing that anyone was on his trail. The only liability Fargo saw was that the backshooter knew the land and might have made a beeline for his hideout where he would feel safe. Nothing in the tracks showed the least hesitation in choosing a path.

Down into a valley and up a steeper slope brought Fargo to a spot where he could see another grassy valley, this one stretching for a mile or more into the Front Range. Trotting down the middle of the valley rode a man trailing a riderless horse. Fargo wasted no time going after him. He had the outlaw in sight.

The man vanished behind a stand of white-barked aspen mixed with ponderosa pines, giving Fargo the chance to gallop ahead and close the distance even more. When he reached the far side of the copse, Fargo reined back. He didn't want to ride into an ambush when the man he trailed had shown how willing he was to murder without even offering quarter.

A small shack stood to one side of the clearing. A faint puff of black smoke belched from the chimney, quickly followed by a thicker cloud.

Fargo pictured what went on inside the shack perfectly, as if he could see through the rickety wood walls. The man started a fire to boil himself some coffee, perhaps a bottle of whiskey sat on a table or shelf and waited to be added to the coffee. Whether the whiskey was there Fargo could only guess, but the backshooter was getting ready for a small celebration of his crimes.

Fargo tethered his Ovaro and then walked to the shack, approaching it from the back. He pressed his ear against the wall and satisfied himself that the killer was alone inside. The two horses in front of the shack had hinted at that, but Fargo wanted to be sure.

He walked around to the front of the cabin, took a deep breath, then kicked in the flimsy wood door. Fargo cocked his Colt and pointed it at the same instant he yelled, "Freeze!"

He had the drop on a surprised Whip Ballinger, seated at the table and counting a roll of greenbacks.

5

"Who are you?" demanded Ballinger. He pushed his chair away from the table, his gun hand twitching slightly as he considered going for the six-gun hanging at his hip.

"Don't try it," Fargo warned, his eyes cold and his hand steady. He had the drop on Ballinger and the gunman was seated, making it difficult to draw and fire.

"I know you. You was the galoot Mr. Austin was talkin' to about huntin' for us. You got me confused with a deer?" Ballinger laughed harshly. He still hadn't figured out Fargo held the winning hand.

"No more than you confused that man you shot in the back of the head with a deer." Fargo stepped through the door and moved to the side so he wouldn't be an outlined target. Whip Ballinger was still deciding whether to make a play since Fargo had him dead to rights for the murder. "You even stole his horse and left his body for the buzzards."

"What's it to you?"

"Unbuckle that gun belt and let it fall," Fargo said. He lifted his Colt and aimed it squarely between Ballinger's eyes, helping him make the right choice. He hastily obeyed and then kicked the six-shooter away when it hit the dirt floor.

"What are you gonna do with me? Was he a friend or something?"

"I didn't know him," Fargo said, picking up the fallen gun belt and slinging it over his shoulder. The six-shooter would be evidence against Ballinger at his trial. "All I know is who you are, you backshooting son of a bitch."

He gestured with his six-gun and got Ballinger moving.
"Where are you takin' me?"
"Back to Nugget to stand trial. I saw a jailhouse, so there must be a town marshal."
"There is," Ballinger said, "but you ain't gonna like it when I tell 'im *you* shot that pilgrim."
Fargo wasn't going to bandy words with the killer. He got Ballinger on his horse, then secured the man's arms around his body with a couple turns from his lariat. Guarding the man as if he watched a hungry cougar, Fargo led Ballinger's horse and the stolen mount to where he had left his Ovaro. In a few minutes they were riding back to town, Fargo never taking his eyes off Ballinger.
When they rode into Nugget it was turning dark, but the sight of Fargo bringing Whip Ballinger in, rope around him and at gunpoint, roused the revelers in the Lucky Nugget. Dozens of men came tumbling out, pointing and whispering excitedly among themselves. Fargo jerked the rope and got Ballinger off his horse in front of the calaboose.
"Inside," Fargo ordered. He never dropped his guard. Ballinger had come along willingly enough, but he might turn and bolt at any instant. He had already shown the kind of man he was.
Ballinger snarled, then kicked the door open with his foot and went in, Fargo trailing. A weaselly looking man looked up from his newspaper when they entered.
"What's goin' on here?" the marshal demanded. "You can't go bangin' down my door like that, Whip. I won't allow it!" After his brief tirade details began working their way into his slow brain. He saw the turns of rope around Ballinger's shoulders and the way Fargo herded him, Colt drawn and ready to shoot.
"I have a prisoner, Marshal," Fargo said. "Ballinger shot a man out on the road in the back of the head, stole his poke and horse, then left the body for the ants."
"Who you talkin' about?" asked the marshal, frowning. This made him look even more like a weasel.
"I don't know the victim's name. He's still on the road

leading to Denver. Ballinger's motive must have been nothing but pure greed and a streak of mean a mile wide."

"Now, Marshal Peterson, you know I'm no killer. It was this gent's doing. He killed that traveler, not me."

"Here's Ballinger's pistol," Fargo said, dropping the gun on the marshal's desk, along with the holster and belt. "It's been fired once. I found him at a cabin a couple miles from the road counting this." He added the roll of greenbacks to the pile on the desk. "The horse he took is outside."

"He got the drop on me. I don't know nuthin' about any of this, Marshal. And sure, I done fired that hogleg. At a rabbit!"

"These are serious charges, Whip. I can't let you go runnin' off if you done like he said you did." The marshal stroked the stubble on his chin, then asked, "You bag the rabbit, Whip? I could do with a little rabbit stew."

Fargo grated his teeth. Marshal Peterson didn't seem too inclined to take the murder charge seriously.

"When can he stand trial, Marshal?" Fargo asked.

"Well, now, that's a poser. Don't rightly know if Judge Serviss is on the circuit this time of year or if he took off to go fishin'."

"Keep him in jail until the judge comes," Fargo said. "From the looks of him he's no great loss."

Marshal Peterson shook his head. "Can't do that. Don't have the funds to feed the varmint more than a day or two."

"You'd let a cold-blooded murderer and horse thief go free?"

"You know the law, mister?" asked the marshal. "A man's innocent till he's proved guilty. Nobody's proved Whip here is guilty of a danged thing."

"Fetch the body. See if it's not the way I said."

"Your word against mine, Fargo," Ballinger said haughtily. "I'm innocent. And I say you're the killer."

"You hush up, Whip. This gent—his name's Fargo?—this gent's got a right to bring charges."

"I want out on bail."

"You don't have any money," Fargo said.

"He's got you there, Whip," Marshal Peterson said. He opened his center desk draw and swept the money taken from the dead man into it. Fargo had the feeling this was no longer evidence but had become part of the marshal's pay.

"Are you going to lock him up?" asked Fargo. He still had his Colt trained on Ballinger. If he had to, he would take Ballinger into Denver City to stand trial. It was a long ride and would be difficult because keeping Ballinger bottled up required constant vigilance.

"Of course I am. What do you take me for?" snapped the marshal. Fargo didn't bother answering. Peterson pushed the coils of rope off Ballinger and shoved him to the rear of thc jailhouse. Two empty cells showed the lack of law enforcement in Nugget.

"Do I have my pick of suites?" drawled Ballinger.

"Get in there, you varmint." Peterson's words were tough, but he made no move to push Ballinger into either cell, letting his prisoner choose for himself. Only when the lock snapped shut did Fargo relax a mite and shove his Colt back into its holster.

"When will he come to trial?" asked Fargo, fearing Peterson was right about the circuit judge taking months to reach Nugget.

"Not too long," Marshal Peterson said vaguely.

"Should I stay in town to testify?"

"Do as you see fit. I got evidence. When we fetch back that body, if we can find it, that ought to be ample for the town prosecutor."

Fargo nodded and left, then stopped and wondered if he ought to ask the marshal who Nugget's prosecutor might be. He shrugged it off. He would find out soon enough, although the marshal had told him he could leave.

The Grafton claim wasn't too far and he had a hankering to see Susanna again, but Fargo decided to pitch camp out in the woods above Nugget. Riding up on the brothers in the dark was a sure way to get his hide ventilated.

An hour past noon found Fargo waiting at the crude gate to the Grafton claim. He sat patiently in the saddle until Zeb Grafton recognized him and decided it was all right to let him advance.

"Come on in, Fargo," Zeb said uneasily. "I ain't sure Ben wants to see you again, but you're about all Susanna talks about."

"Not about the gold?" Fargo said, grinning. He had spent a fair amount of time thinking about the petite beauty, too.

"Well, she does go on about how rich we're gettin', but you get mentioned a lot, too."

"When did you put up the gate?" Fargo indicated the two posts holding the crude swinging gate across the path. The Graftons had not bothered putting up a fence on either side, making the gate more symbolic than useful.

"Right after we hit it big," Zeb said proudly. He looked over his shoulder and licked his lips nervously. "You got business or you just visitin'?"

"Call it a social visit."

"Ben doesn't want you sniffin' around our sister, no matter what she says."

"I'll let Susanna decide that for herself," Fargo said, dismounting. He walked up the ruts toward the claim. A dozen yards away Ben crouched at the edge of the river, avidly panning for gold. He sloshed the pan around so fast, Fargo wondered if he didn't spill out most of the contents, gold and dross together.

"Sis is up at the campsite," Zeb said, increasingly nervous. "Don't let on I seen you, Fargo. Not to Ben. He's mighty touchy 'bout purty near everything now."

"I understand," Fargo said. The lure of gold turned decent men into monsters. Having a strike as rich as this one appeared required constant vigilance against claim-jumpers. Fargo could see how Ben thought he might be trying to marry rich by romancing Susanna.

Zeb looked grateful, then went down the path to the river and joined his brother in their hunt for the elusive wealth hidden by nature. Fargo went to the camp where Susanna boiled a pot of beans and struggled to knead a large lump of dough. A Dutch oven was ready for it when she finished. The brunette looked up and a smile lighted her face when she saw him. Susanna wiped her hands on her apron and stood.

"Skye! I didn't think I'd see you again!" She rushed over and hugged him tightly. The small woman looked up at him, her expression changing subtly. Fargo knew the beans would burn and the bread would go unbaked if he gave her the slightest sign.

"I might have to stay around for a while," he said. It took a few minutes to explain how he had brought Whip Ballinger in for the unknown man's murder.

"That's terrible, thinking such a horrid killer calls Nugget his home." Susanna shivered a little. "It's good having a man like you around to protect us—and everyone in town. You should be the marshal."

"That'd tie me down too much," Fargo said honestly. "How are you doing? You seem to have plenty of supplies now. Have your brothers mined enough to pay for all this?"

"They panned out an incredible amount of gold in only a day," Susanna said. Something in her tone told Fargo there was more to it. He held his tongue until she explained. "We signed an IOU at the general store."

"For how much?"

"A thousand."

"What? What did you buy? Oysters and cases of champagne?" He looked around the camp and wondered how anything smaller than an entire wagon could cost so much.

"This is the frontier, Skye. We bought staples to keep us going for a few weeks. Things cost more, lots more," she said, as if repeating what the storekeeper had said. "With the note at the bank, we owe over two thousand dollars."

"That much?" Fargo shook his head. "Did Ben use

the gold he's already panned to pay off some of the debt?" From Susanna's expression, he realized the gold had already been paid out. This mountain of crushing debt was in addition to the value of the metal already recovered from the river.

"Don't fret, Skye. It'll be fine," Susanna said brightly. "The river's filled with gold. Ben and Zeb are hard workers and will get it out, and we'll be rich."

"What will you do then? Return to St. Louis?"

"Oh, perhaps, unless I found something—someone—who could persuade me stay here," Susanna said, grinning wickedly at Fargo. There was no mistaking her meaning.

"What the hell are you doin' here?" came the unexpected angry words. Fargo turned and looked over his shoulder. A wet Ben Grafton slogged up the path from the river. "Didn't you see the gate? This is posted property, Fargo."

"Oh, Ben, calm down. Skye was just paying his respects."

"He's here to jump our claim!"

"How much gold have you found today?" Fargo asked. "Any more nuggets the size of the one yesterday?"

"We haven't panned near as much today," Ben admitted reluctantly. "But we will. The nugget proves there's more in the river, lots more! And none of it is yours!"

Fargo wondered if Ben and Zeb had found even one more speck of gold but said nothing.

"I invited him to stay for supper," Susanna said.

Before Ben could start an argument no one would win, Fargo said, "I was just telling your sister I had to get back to Nugget. Important business."

"Don't let the gate hit you in the butt as you leave," Ben said. He meant it to sound tough, but Fargo fought hard to keep from laughing. The gate was a joke, and Ben Grafton wasn't likely to throw anyone off his claim who wanted to stay.

"Don't be rude, Ben. I want Skye to stay."

"That's all right, Miss Grafton," Fargo said formally. "I'll come back to see you before I head for Denver."

Susanna's lips thinned, and she looked daggers at her brother. But neither of them said a word as Fargo mounted and rode away from the Grafton camp. He rode around the gate and then decided to explore the countryside rather than return to Nugget, where sitting in the saloon and drinking was his only likely diversion.

As he rode, Fargo saw occasional dirt trails leading in the direction of the river. He counted no fewer than a dozen, indicating many prospectors were working the stream above the Grafton claim. This reduced the brothers' chances of finding gold, although they had hit it rich already. Fargo thought about inquiring of the other miners about their own luck in finding color amid the water-smoothed stones in the river but decided against it. Having wild-eyed, gold-dazed miners taking potshots at him was something he would reserve for later when life got too dull.

Riding away from the river took Fargo through a maze of mining roads leading to hard rock mines painstakingly scrabbled from the side of the mountain. Tailings showed the mines had been worked for months. Fargo considered how much more the Grafton brothers might make logging and then cutting supports for the mine tunnels. Timber was plentiful and miners would pay top dollar not to waste precious time sawing wood.

He determined at least forty claims dotted the hills and lined the river where Ben and Zeb had chosen to make their fortune. The odds against them appeared increasingly dim, but they were optimistic. Sometimes that was enough.

Sometimes.

Fargo found himself back on the road leading to Denver City. He looked downhill and felt a pull to return to Denver, then go north into Wyoming. The green meadows and abundant game there called to him like a siren, but he had obligations in Nugget. In spite of what Marshal Peterson said about him being free to leave, Fargo wanted to testify against Ballinger to be certain justice was done.

He turned his Ovaro back toward town when he heard

the loud snap of a whip and the rattle of chains and creak of wood. Fargo dismounted and waited as a light wagon pulled by a dozen mules slowly worked its way up the road.

"What're you doin' out here, Fargo?" came the prickly question. "Can't get rid of you, no matter where I go."

"Still mistreating your mules, I see," Fargo said, returning Clem Parson's greeting in kind. The last thing in the world Parson would do was harm one of his precious mules. The muleteer thought more of the sturdy, dependable animals than he did of the often-drunk drivers he hired to drive his other wagons.

"Get your worthless hide over here so I can take some of it off with my bullwhacker!" Parson flicked the whip expertly, cracking it a few feet in front of Fargo.

"You hauling freight to Nugget?"

"I needed the work," Parson said, setting his brake and jumping down. "The mules need a rest," he said in way of explanation why he stopped to palaver with Fargo.

"You delivering goods to Harry Austin?"

"Who else? The coyote owns the whole danged mountain. Nugget is his, lock, stock, and barrel. And *I* brought him some more barrels."

Fargo saw barrels of flour and other dry goods in the rear of the wagon.

"That's enough food for a couple hundred folks," Fargo observed.

"I'm in front of a real storm of prospectors coming up from Denver. They caught wind of the big strike and are flockin' here. Lots of money to be made, Fargo. You want to come work for me? I can pay top dollar."

"Thanks, Parson," the Trailsman answered, "but I've got other irons in the fire."

"That pretty little filly you rescued out on the prairie, eh?" Parson nodded knowingly, then added. "You're not the kind to get tied to apron strings, Fargo. Watch yourself."

Fargo laughed. He knew that Susanna wanted more than a quick tumble in the hay.

"No need to put me on the payroll, but I'll help you unload your cargo in Nugget."

"I'll buy you the best meal in town."

"That might not be much more than a plate of beans," Fargo said.

"That good, eh?" Parson slapped Fargo on the shoulder, then climbed back into the driver's box, got his mules pulling, and then released the brake. The wagon shot forward. Fargo rode beside Parson, catching up on news from Denver. It took the rest of the day to reach Nugget. By the time Parson halted his team, it was past seven.

"Everything's closed up tight, 'cept for the saloon," Parson said. "Reckon we can find food there."

"I knew you'd find a way to do me out of the meal," Fargo said.

"You haven't done anything but ride, yet," Parson said irritably. They found themselves a table at the corner of the Lucky Nugget and swapped tall tales about freighting and hunting as they ate. An hour later, a flood of men poured into the saloon.

"The new prospectors. I kin smell 'em, and I don't mean stale sweat," said Parson. "They're such greenhorns, they're all but beggin' to be rooked."

Fargo thought of the Graftons and agreed with the freighter. He felt uneasy at the way they had struck it big so fast—and the way Ben and Zeb hadn't located much gold since. The brothers were up to their ears in debt to Harry Austin, and Fargo suspected the rest of the newcomers would soon be, also.

"I got a bit of mail and documents Austin wants me to deliver back in Denver. This might be a lucrative route for a postrider. Austin sends danged near as much mail down as he orders supplies up the hill."

"Quit trying to fix me up with a job," Fargo said. He considered what Parson said. "What kind of mail? A prospector's not going to spend any time writing home, not when there's gold to be scratched out of the ground."

"Most all of it's Austin's," Parson said. "I swear he sends tons, or so it seems. If you don't want to be a postrider, Byers at the *News* is looking for someone to deliver newspapers. Pay is good and you get to be in the hot, burning sun all the time, since that seems what you want out of life."

The ribbing was good-natured, and Fargo started to reply in kind when he overheard two men's loud conversation as they came into the Lucky Nugget.

"Excuse me a minute," Fargo said to Parson, going after the men. He pushed through the growing crowd to stop them. "What's that I heard you say about an accident?" His heart pounded at what he was afraid he would hear.

"A fellow pannin' for gold outside town. Me'n my pardner fished him out of the river dead as a doornail." The miner wiped his hands on his dirty canvas trousers and looked longingly toward the bar. He would talk a man's ear off all night long, but first he wanted a shot of whiskey to wet his whistle.

"You didn't get his name?"

"Nope, sure didn't 'cause he was dead," the miner said. "Took his body back to his camp. All I know for sure is he's got a brother and 'bout the purtiest sister I ever set eyes on. If she wants to get married, I'd take real good care of—"

Fargo didn't bother listening to the rest. He was already on his way out of the saloon, bound for the Grafton claim.

6

Fargo shook his head at the pathetic gate as he rode through it and went directly to the Graftons' campsite. Although it was after midnight, a fire flared high and sent dancing, twisting sparks into the cold night air. Two figures crouched close together on the far side of the blaze.

"Susanna," Fargo called. He jumped to the ground and hurried to the fire. One of the dim figures looked up. The fire illuminated the woman's face fully as Susanna moved. Tears left dusty tracks down her cheeks, and he had never seen her so distraught. If there had been any question who had died, her tormented face told him the facts.

Her brother Zeb stood and held her close when she tried to rush to him. She fought for a moment and then relented, remaining in Zeb's embrace.

"We don't need nuthin' from the likes of you," Zeb said in a weak parody of his brother.

"What happened to Ben?" Fargo ignored the young man entirely. Susanna was in charge and always had been, even when Ben's greed had run wild because of their gold strike.

"I . . . we don't know. Not exactly. Ben was down on the river. He might have been working his way out to the middle to see if he could spot more gold there. Some other prospectors found his body more than a mile downstream."

"Where is he? His body?" Fargo hated to be so blunt,

but he had to find out the truth. Nothing was as it appeared in Nugget, and Ben's death might not have been an accident. It worried him that the only ones who profited stood in front of him now, but he could not imagine either Susanna or Zeb killing their brother.

"D-down by the river," Zeb got out.

"Look after her until I get back," Fargo ordered, to give Zeb something to do and to keep him out of his hair. He made his way down the slippery, muddy path to the riverbank. The thin sliver of rising moon illuminated the area enough for him to spot the dark shape near where he had seen Ben panning earlier. Fargo knelt and rolled over the body. He turned Ben's head from side to side, looking at the elongated wound on the man's head. Something large and heavy had crushed the back of his head, as if he had been clubbed.

Fargo stood and stared at the middle of the fast-running river. Ben could have lost his balance trying to wade out there, been swept downstream, and hit the back of his head on a submerged rock. If he had been carried a mile, the rock that had crushed the life from him might be anywhere. Even a man of Fargo's ability might never find it because the swift flow of water would wash away all traces of blood.

Or Ben Grafton might have been hit from the rear and his body tossed into the water. Fargo had no way of declaring this to be a murder and knew the truth might never come out. With the rapid influx of prospectors and news of the Grafton claim being a rich one, any of the town's newcomers might be suspects. Or any of those farther downstream, who thought Ben might be stealing their precious gold.

Fargo looked upstream and knew even those men might be lured into murder for gold.

Or it could be an unfortunate accident caused by Ben's zealous pursuit of gold in the middle of a treacherous river.

"What do you think, Skye?" came Susanna's quavering voice.

"I think you should get back to camp, where I told you to stay." He moved to block her view of the body.

"I saw him when they brought him into camp. Two men from farther downstream. Th-they were upset over it. They—" Susanna burst into tears and rushed toward him. Her arms circled his body as she buried her face in his chest. Fargo held her tight and kept quiet because words meant nothing now. He had seen his share of death on the frontier and had comforted sisters and wives and families and had never learned the right words that would make it better.

"We have to bury him," he said when the petite woman's sobs had eased a mite. "Leaving him on the bank like this will attract coyotes." Fargo felt Susanna stiffen at such callous words, but she had to face the reality of her brother's death. There was no time for mourning until the distasteful duties were past.

"I can get Zeb to help. A spot up above our camp would be nice, so he can look down on the river and our claim," Susanna said.

"You and Zeb don't need to bother yourselves. I can dig the grave. But if you want to say a few words—"

"No!" Susanna was adamant. "Ben's our brother. We have to do what we can. It's bad enough there's no preacher in Nugget to say a benediction over his grave."

The number of funerals Fargo had attended amounted to dozens and only twice had the dead been buried in a cemetery where a preacher conducted the ceremony, most recently when his buddy 'Rone Clawson had been shot. The rest had been laid to rest under the sky and stars where the deceased had to make his own peace.

Fargo pushed Susanna away gently and said, "Get shovels and take them to the spot where you want Ben buried." He waited for her to go back to camp before he knelt, grunted, and heaved the corpse up across his broad shoulders. Fargo took a few tentative steps, got the weight settled, and began trudging up the hill toward what would be a new grave site.

* * *

They sat around the dying fire, each wrapped in thought. Fargo eyed Susanna and saw how disconsolate she was. But Zeb was another matter. The young man had a set to his jaw that Fargo did not like. It was the way a man who had come to a decision looked. Ben Grafton's burial had been short and quick, with Susanna singing a hymn and Zeb saying a few words. But Susanna's grief had not changed. Zeb's had.

"You should sell the claim," Fargo said to Susanna, but he watched Zeb closely. The way the young man bristled reminded Fargo more of Ben Grafton.

"No!" Zeb shouted, slamming his hand down on the ground next to him. "Ben wouldn't like it. Ben wanted us to be rich, and this is the claim that'll do it!"

"Can you pan enough to get yourself out of debt?" Fargo asked. "If you sell, there are a dozen prospectors new to Nugget that might buy."

"We couldn't get enough to pay off Mr. Austin," Susanna said. "Zeb's right. We have to keep working the claim. If not in Ben's memory, then to pay our lawful debt."

Fargo admired her spirit but knew it would keep her in bondage to this claim for the rest of her life. Zeb was nowhere as good at panning as his brother, and Ben had not been that good.

"Will you find enough gold to stay ahead of new debts?" Fargo asked. "I don't think so."

"Ben was right about you. You want to jump our claim," Zeb said.

"Hush up, Zeb," Susanna said. "Skye wants what is best for us." She turned. He saw the way she straightened her shoulders and knew what she would say before the words came from her delicately sculpted lips. "We owe it to Ben's memory. We will not sell!"

"There's not much more I can do," he said, standing. "I wish you the best."

"Wait, Skye. Where are you going?"

"Back to Denver. From there, I don't rightly know."

"Don't go, not yet. Please stay, at least for a while. For me."

Fargo felt the tug at his duty. He had rescued the Graftons out on the prairie and felt an obligation to do what he could to help Susanna and her surviving brother. But what could he do? He was no miner and had no stake in their panning operation.

Fargo worried over the answer and kept coming back to the condition of Ben Grafton's body. It had taken some damage during the wild ride downstream, but the head wound had been deep in the skull. The bone had been smashed as if a long, thin rod had crashed into the back of Ben's head rather than a broad, river-smoothed rock. That bothered him, but since he had not seen the deadly blow, Ben might have bashed his head against a floating tree limb rather than a rock.

Still, the uncertainty ate away at Fargo's gut. Something was not right. He might never find out the truth, but he had to try. He owed that much to Susanna—and to her brother.

"Try to get some sleep," he told her. "I want to scout along the river and see if I can find where Ben hit his head."

"That's a fool's errand," said Zeb. He sounded more and more like his dead brother with every passing minute.

Fargo ignored him, held Susanna for a moment, then went to see what he could find. The moon was high but shone down with a silvery gleam occasionally dulled by thin clouds. Fargo knew he had a better chance of finding any sign of a crime in full daylight, but he wanted to stay out of the Grafton camp, at least for a few hours. Zeb and Susanna had to work out their problems between themselves. An outsider would only enflame already raw nerves.

Walking slowly, Fargo hunted for the spot where Ben had left the bank and gone into the raging river. The slick rocks and gravel prevented any hope of finding the man's tracks, much less where he had waded out in his search for more flecks of gold on the river bottom. A half mile of walking accomplished nothing, so Fargo found a rock looking out over the river and settled down to think.

His mind spun out of control, not focusing on anything in particular. He laid back, hands behind his head as he stared at the stars and the fingernail of moon. The rush of the river drowned out any sound from the surrounding woods and lulled him into a half sleep. Fargo sat up fast when an unexpectedly loud sound rose above the river's lullaby.

"Dammit," came the curse. "I almost busted my ankle."

"Shut up and bring me the bag."

Fargo recognized the second voice but not the first. He slid across the rock to see what Harry Austin was doing on the riverbank at this time of night. Scuttling like a lizard brought him to the edge of the rock where he could look down on Austin and another man tussling with a large burlap bag. He tried to carry it on his shoulder, but it always managed to get away from him, forcing the man to drop it and heave it back into place.

"Give me three or four of the small ones," Austin said.

The man accompanying the owner of Nugget grumbled and dropped the bag. He rummaged about inside and handed Austin something small. Austin tossed the dark pieces into the river at his feet.

The pair moved on, rounding a bend in the river. Fargo jumped down from his vantage point and went to where Austin had paused. On hands and knees, he looked in the stream. Glints off a rock caught his eye. Fargo fished out the stone and held it up so the moonlight reflected from it.

"Gold," he said. It was hard telling for certain, but Fargo had seen enough, both day and night, to identify the precious metal. He tucked the nugget into his pocket, then paused to consider what he had seen.

Austin was salting the banks. But Fargo could neither prove it to the authorities nor the Graftons. Austin could claim the found nugget was legitimate if Fargo tried to accuse the man of any crime.

Fargo hastily rounded the bend in the river to see if he could catch Austin and his henchman. His hand flashed to his six-shooter when a shotgun blast sounded.

Fargo retreated a step and then advanced cautiously and saw in the distance Austin standing on a small sandbar. He held something in his hand, but it wasn't a shotgun. Fargo had heard enough shells fired in his day to recognize the distinctive sound.

Austin moved off the sandbar, opened his coat, and tucked whatever he was holding away in his waistband.

"Come on. We've got a few more places to visit."

"You're like the damned tooth fairy," grumbled the man, still struggling with the heavy burlap bag.

"I'm better, much better," laughed Austin. The two men went off, again leaving Fargo far behind. He waited until they vanished, then walked out on the sandbar and stared at the gravel just under the water.

The spot shone as if a shattered mirror had been tossed down. Fargo scooped up a handful of the sand and let it slip through his fingers. The bright specks in the cascading wet sand were gold, tiny particles worth several dollars.

Instead of confronting Austin, Fargo retraced his tracks to the Graftons' camp. To his relief Susanna had fallen into a troubled sleep, but Zeb sat up as if guarding his sister.

"You weren't gone long," Zeb said. Fargo read the completion of the man's sentiment. *Not gone long enough,* was what Zeb actually meant.

"I saw something that might interest you," Fargo said, sitting down a respectful distance from Zeb.

"You found where Ben went under?"

"No," Fargo admitted. "but I saw Harry Austin salting the river. He dropped this into the shallows." Fargo pulled out the nugget Austin had left and tossed it to Zeb. The young man caught it clumsily and held it up. His eyes widened when he saw the streaks of gold shot through the drossy rock.

"This is worth ten or twenty dollars!"

"Austin salted it for someone else to find. Just like he put the nugget Ben found into the river."

"You don't know what you're saying, Fargo," Zeb said

angrily. "You want to steal our gold, that's all. You think you can lie about Mr. Austin and run us off."

"Why would I lie about him?"

"He's been real good to us, me and Sis and Ben. He loaned us a passel of money. He believes in us. You don't. All you're out to do is steal our gold."

Zeb muttered something else under his breath that Fargo couldn't hear, but it didn't matter. He knew the young man intended to remain at the claim, working until his fingers were bloody from moving rocks. Another problem vexed Fargo. He knew the land was being salted and was worthless. Even if the Graftons did come to their senses, how could he stand by and let them sell their property to another victim of Harry Austin's scheme? That would compound the crimes being perpetrated.

He felt an obligation toward Susanna and Zeb, but condoning the sale of property he knew was worthless made him an accomplice to fraud. He would never do that.

There had to be a way out. All Fargo had to do was find it.

7

Fargo had breakfast cooked by the time Susanna and Zeb awoke. He scooped some of the bacon out of the frying pan and passed it to Susanna, who rubbed her eyes, then took it gratefully.

"I'm not the best cook in the world, so it might not be to your liking."

"It is," she said.

"You haven't tasted it yet," he said.

"I don't have to. I didn't have to fix it. That makes it perfect." Susanna smiled and the sun came up all over again. Zeb's expression was stormier, but Fargo ignored it as he worked on his own breakfast. He wished they had eggs to go with the bacon, but he hadn't seen a single chicken since coming to Nugget. That would change when enough miners came in and demanded a decent meal in town now and then to take the edge off their backbreaking work.

This line of thought brought him back to the Graftons and what to do about their claim.

Zeb spoke up before Fargo could broach the subject.

"I can't take enough gold from the stream by myself," he stated flatly. Fargo held his peace since he sensed Zeb was building up to something more. The young man heaved a deep breath and plunged on. "I thought maybe you could help out, Sis, but that wouldn't be right. Ben wouldn't like it."

"I can help," Susanna said, but her heart wasn't in it.

"You help out plenty doing the cooking and laundry,"

Zeb said, his eyes a bit glazed as he worked on his grandiose plans. "I need to build a rocker. With it doing most of the sifting work, I can shovel in as much sand and pay dirt as Ben and I'd've taken out in a day."

"You don't have the equipment available in Nugget," Fargo said, seeing a way of winning some time so he could come up with a better plan. "You'll have to go to Denver."

"Then that's where I'll go," Zeb said with more assurance than good sense.

Susanna looked from her brother to Fargo. Her limpid ginger eyes fixed on him, almost accusingly.

"Why can't we find the parts for this rocker here in Nugget?"

"Metal parts," Fargo said hastily. It would take Zeb a couple days to reach Denver, another to buy the pieces of mining equipment and maybe three more to return. A week ought to be enough for him to find the true depths of Harry Austin's treachery.

From there, Fargo could decide what to do. If Austin sold the property after salting it, he could be arrested and Susanna and Zeb might get their money back—or some of it. Fargo realized it was a big leap from seeing Austin strolling along the riverbank and proving the man was running an elaborate scheme, but so many of Austin's actions screamed "illegal!"

"Will this speed up the work?" Susanna asked Zeb.

"I seen plans for a rocker like the ones used out in California. I can build one."

"We don't have any money, and Mr. Austin is the only one who'll loan us money," she pointed out.

Fargo sucked in his breath, then said, "I can loan you twenty dollars. That ought to be enough to buy the steel braces, nails, and other things you can't get here."

Zeb looked at him suspiciously, but his need to prove the claim was greater than his distrust. Fargo handed over half of all the money he had earned scouting for Clem Parson, but he thought it was money well spent if it kept Zeb out of his hair for a week. By the time the young man returned, Austin would be behind bars and

Susanna would have the money paid out for the claim back. As for the rest, the money spent for supplies and for the original map back in St. Louis, Fargo had no hope of recovering any of that.

"I better get going," Zeb said. "It's a long walk, and I have to take an ox to carry back the supplies."

Fargo watched Susanna help Zeb prepare a burlap sack of food for his trip. Zeb glared at him as he led an ox out of the camp, then stopped and said in a voice too low for Susanna to overhear, "You touch my sister, and I swear I'll cut your heart out!"

"I'll see that she's safe while you're gone," Fargo said. Zeb might think it was his duty now to look after his older sister, but that was Susanna's business. Fargo would promise that no harm would come to her, but he felt a stirring down low that told him he might share a blanket with the lovely woman again. If he did, that would be between the two of them and nobody else.

Zeb grunted and knew he had no chance against Fargo. He still tried to look like a bravo as he led the lumbering ox from camp and down the road leading to Denver.

"Why did you want to get rid of him, Skye? To be with me?" Susanna smiled weakly, but she had too much on her mind for dalliance at the moment. Her other brother had just died and his death weighed heavily on her.

Fargo told her what he had seen the night before and how he suspected Harry Austin of salting the claims.

"You think it is all a hoax?"

"From the map in St. Louis to the nugget Ben found," Fargo said, nodding grimly. "Austin sends a powerful lot of mail out. I think it might be new treasure maps showing different parts of the mountainside around Nugget."

"His accomplices sell the maps for what they can get, the dupes come out here and then Austin cons them—us—into buying a bogus stretch of barren, worthless rock?"

Fargo said nothing. That summed up his conclusion well. Austin didn't care if he collected anything from the men selling the maps. He conned those foolish enough to make the trip and pay inflated prices at his general store and take out usurious loans with his bank. If enough men bragged about finding gold in the river, this primed the pump for even more prospectors to buy from his stores.

"I don't know, Skye. Really," Susanna said, obviously torn. "Ben was so sure he had hit it big here. Zeb thinks so, too."

"Zeb doesn't want to admit his brother was wrong. And Ben was dazzled by the gleam of gold. It happens." He studied Susanna closely. It had happened to her, too. The lure of quick wealth was always too hard to resist, especially for a family like the Graftons, cut loose from their roots.

Fargo started to tell the woman of his suspicion that Ben might have been murdered, but he held back. There was no reason to burden her further. She had plenty to mull over.

"I'll help get the plates clean and—" Fargo froze, cocked his head to one side and strained to hear.

"What's wrong?" Susanna asked. He silenced her with the wave of a hand.

Fargo knew the sound of a gunshot when he heard one. It was distant, echoing along the valley where the river rushed, and almost drowned by the noise of the racing water. The report might have been imagined, but Fargo didn't think so.

"I need to check something out," he told her.

"What, Skye? I didn't hear anything."

He saddled his Ovaro and was halfway to the lonely gate before he answered.

"Stay here and keep a sharp eye out. You've got a six-shooter. Use it if anyone else comes."

He galloped hard, then slowed his horse and finally let it rest so he could listen for new sounds. He had learned to classify sounds early on in the wilderness. Fargo knew the difference between thunder, a tree limb snapping, and a gunshot. From a great enough distance, most men could not tell them apart.

The Trailsman could. He rode down the road less than a hundred yards before he stopped.

"No," he groaned, seeing the body sprawled in the middle of the road. Zeb's ox munched grass at the shoulder, uncaring that its master had been gunned down.

Fargo hit the ground running and dropped to the young man's side. Zeb lay facedown. Fargo expected to see the single shot in the back of his head but only dirt greeted his examination. He rolled Zeb onto his back and found the bullet wound. Fargo ripped open Zeb's shirt and saw how lucky the young man had been. The bullet had entered his right side and bounced along his lower rib and exited in the back, leaving a clean wound.

But what might be damaged inside? Zeb bled sluggishly from both the entry and exit wounds. Fargo used the man's shirt to wipe away what dirt he could and then bound the gunshot holes.

"Shot me," groaned Zeb. He thrashed weakly.

"Stay still," Fargo said sharply. "I'll get you back to camp. Susanna can take care of you there." He wondered if Zeb could stand, then saw how weak the man was. "Did you see who shot you?"

From the angle of the wound, Zeb had been shot by someone off to one side of the road, possibly hiding in a clump of bushes. His shirt pocket had been ripped off and the twenty dollars Fargo had given him was missing.

Fargo was pretty sure the tracks that the thief left behind belonged to Ballinger's horse. How the man had escaped Fargo couldn't say, but there was no time to track the varmint down and find out, he had to see to Zeb first. He got his arm around the man's shoulders, then grabbed his belt and dragged him to his feet. Zeb moaned and almost passed out but gamely let Fargo steer him toward the ox. Fargo boosted him up and belly-down over the animal's back.

From there it was a slow, tedious trip back to the Grafton camp. All the way Fargo dreaded arriving because he had to tell Susanna her only living brother was in a bad way and might not live out the day.

* * *

"He's burning up, Skye. I don't know what more to do for him," Susanna said, wringing her hands in worry. She stared at Zeb, who lay pallid and unmoving on the blankets Fargo had spread for him under the wagon to keep him out of the sun.

"Keep a damp cloth on his forehead," Fargo said. "I'll go into Nugget and get some medicine. I didn't see a doctor's office, but someone has to know how to patch up a gunshot."

"The wound's fine. Infection's setting in."

Fargo knew she was right. He wished he knew the country better. If a Ute or Cheyenne camp was near, he could get their medicine man to whip up a potion. The Indians had better luck curing their ills than the white man did with fancy bottles of foul-tasting medicines.

"I never noticed if there was a barber in town. He might be able to bleed Zeb," Susanna said anxiously.

"That's not what Zeb needs." Fargo did not cotton to such methods of healing. They left the patient weaker and worse off than before the treatment.

"He needs something, Skye. He's dying by inches. I can't stand to see him fade away like this." She fought to hold back tears.

Susanna hugged him. Fargo held her for a moment, then gently pushed her away.

"I'll do what I can. You stay with him."

"If he dies, promise me you'll find the killer. If you don't, I swear I'll track him down and scratch his eyes out myself!"

"Zeb won't die," Fargo assured her with more confidence than he felt. He kissed her quickly, then mounted and rode to Nugget to find anyone who could prepare medicine for the fever-ridden Zeb Grafton.

"I do some doctorin'," said the fast-talking Lucky Nugget barkeep. "Mostly, I per-scribe a shot of whiskey fer what ails you." He thumped a bottle of cheap whiskey down on the bar in front of Fargo. "That's fifty dollars for the bottle."

"Fifty?" Fargo stared at the amber liquid and wondered how it had been brewed. Grain alcohol with gunpowder and rusty nails in it for color was the usual recipe for trade whiskey. But the price was outrageous.

"Look around the room," the barkeep said proudly. "We got real business now. Not like you seen a couple days ago."

The bartender's arm swept across the crowded saloon, showing men eager to spend and drink and catch the slightest rumor about gold strikes. Nugget had turned into the kind of town Fargo preferred to avoid. Not only was it getting too loud and crowded, the tenor had changed from one of wariness to stark greed.

"I need a real doctor. There's not one in town?"

"Can't say there is. Denver City's the nearest. What's the problem?" the barkeep asked. His attention was quickly pulled away from Fargo's request when a couple of burly miners banged on the bar demanding beer. Fargo didn't stop the man from doing his job. He turned, forced his way through the crush of prospectors and finally reached the cool, clean air of Nugget's main street. Fargo hardly noticed the dust cloud hanging over the dirt thoroughfare after the heavy smoke and reek inside the saloon.

Fargo was not sure Zeb would survive a trip to Denver, not in his feverish condition. The barkeep had been Fargo's best bet for locating a doctor. That left him with the long shot of the chemist at the assay office. He dodged a galloping horse and a man drunkenly driving a wagon down the middle of the street and ducked into the small shack that served double duty as both assay and land office.

The assayer worked at a wooden bench, pouring liquid into a beaker where it immediately turned a clear blue. The man set down the beaker and shucked off rubber gloves, wiped his nose, then turned to Fargo.

"What can I do for you? I'm real busy."

Fargo explained Zeb's condition and asked, "Is there anything you can do for it? Without a sawbones in town, I'm afraid Zeb'll die unless something is done fast."

"Fever, eh?" The chemist pursed his lips. "I'm no doctor, but I rode with a traveling medicine show for well nigh a year."

"Snake oil?" Fargo asked dubiously.

"That was mostly what they sold, except for a couple medicines they stole from a doctor at some fancy-ass hospital back East. Let me think." The chemist frowned, then went to the bench and started taking down small vials and adding drops from each, mixing the result in a bowl. He finished with a grainy white powder, ground it fine with a mortar and stone pestle, then scraped the flourlike residue into an envelope.

The chemist licked the tip of his finger and dipped it into the powder. He made a face.

"Bitter. Tastes worse than I thought, but it might just work. Kill or cure," he said, dropping it on the counter.

"What is it?" asked Fargo.

"Does it matter? Got a little of this and a little of that in it. Ten dollars."

Fargo knew better than to argue. Zeb was in a bad way and might die even if this concoction helped. He used half of his remaining money to pay the chemist. The ten-dollar gold piece rang like a small, clear bell on the counter.

"Give it in a glass of water. No liquor with it," warned the chemist.

"Thanks."

"Let me know how it works. If your friend pulls through, I might make more money pretending to be a pharmacist than I am working for Mr. Austin as an assayer."

Fargo had nothing to say to that. No one in Nugget did anything out of the goodness of their heart. Money reigned supreme.

He shook his head as he realized how wrong that was. Money was not king. Gold was.

8

Zeb choked as he tried to swallow the white powder Fargo had dissolved in the cup of water.

"What's it? Tastes awful," the young man gasped.

"Don't spit it out," Fargo cautioned, but he spoke to a man who had lapsed back into unconsciousness. The brief escape from the heated grip of the fever showed Zeb was fighting, but it took more than spirit to triumph now.

"Will he get better?" asked Susanna, looking with concern at her brother.

"We ought to know in a few hours. The chemist thought it would help." Fargo touched his shirt pocket. His poke was ten dollars lighter, but the money had been well spent if it broke Zeb's fever. Susanna replaced the damp cloth on her brother's forehead, then edged out from under the wagon.

"I don't know what to do, Skye," she said. "While you werc gone I sat and watched Zeb and actually thought of pulling out, going back to Denver, maybe even returning to St. Louis."

"But?" He heard more in her voice than resignation and capitulation.

"Ben died here. He was sure there was gold in the stream, and I'm like him in one respect. I'm no quitter, either. Even if the streams are bare like you said, Austin owns us until we can do something about it. I can't run and let a bank debt chase Zeb and me around wherever we go."

Fargo knew her dilemma but sometimes the hand you

were dealt was not good enough to win the pot. You had to know when to fold and walk away, especially when others in the game played with a marked deck.

Or you could bluff.

Fargo stroked over his beard as he thought about that. Susanna jolted him out of his reflections.

"You are so good to stay, Skye, but you don't have to. You can go."

"I'm not a quitter, either," Fargo said. "Watch him carefully. Give him plenty of water."

"Where are you going?" she asked. "You said you—"

"I'll be back. I promise," he said. "I've got to find someone for a little palaver." Fargo was glad Susanna did not press him. He wanted to unearth Ballinger and settle the matter of the man robbing prospectors on the road to Nugget. More than this, Fargo had to find out if Ballinger was responsible for gunning down Zeb.

Austin robbed the miners with his exorbitant prices and Ballinger took what Austin did not at gunpoint on the road. It was a sweet setup—and Fargo was going to put an end to it.

Fargo stepped into the street, looked around and went cold inside. His hand slid toward the Colt at his hip, but he did not draw. Walking quickly to the jail, he lifted the latch and kicked in the door.

Marshal Peterson looked up, eyes wide at the intrusion.

"What is it with you sonsabitches?" the marshal said angrily. "Were you raised in a barn and you don't know how to open a door like civilized folks?"

"It seems your prisoner's escaped," Fargo said. His eyes darted to the rear of the jailhouse. Both cell doors stood open.

"Whip didn't escape. He made bail."

"Bail for shooting a man in the back of the head, then robbing him and stealing his horse?" Fargo tried to hold down his anger.

"He got a right. And he met bail."

"Who set the amount? How much was it?" Fargo did

not really want to hear the marshal's reply because he knew it would make him even madder. And it did.

"Settin' bail's up to me since judges are scarcer'n hen's teeth in these here parts. Whip's a fine upstanding citizen of the town of Nugget and not likely to hightail it, so I figgered sixty dollars was good enough."

"You let a murderer go free for that little?"

"You ain't got no call tellin' me how to do my job. Things are peaceable enough in town. Now, I might take it into my head to toss you in the clink if you go kickin' in doors like that anymore."

Fargo held his rage in check. Otherwise, he might be guilty of killing a lawman. Letting Ballinger go free had to be like throwing a bull terrier into a pit with rats. There'd soon be a whole lot of blood and death everywhere.

Fargo took a deep breath, knew he had reached the end of the trail here, turned and left before he said something he would regret. If Whip Ballinger had been out of jail for a day—and maybe longer since Fargo wasn't sure the marshal told the truth—he definitely could have shot Zeb Grafton.

He even could have had something to do with Ben's death.

"Step right up, gents. It's my privilege to announce a special, only for you! Buy ten pounds of flour and beans and get a free drink at the Lucky Nugget!" Harry Austin stood on a crate in front of his general store striking a pose like an orator on the stump. The supplies Clem Parson had freighted in from Denver were stacked high just inside the mercantile's front door. Austin's announcement was met with a roar of approval from the new prospectors who had flooded into town.

"There you go, my good sir," Austin said cheerfully, taking a handful of greenbacks from a man dressed in brand-new clothes. "That's the best ten dollars you ever spent."

"You're charging that much for only flour and beans?" marveled Fargo.

"Mr. Fargo! This is a special promotion. I've reduced the price on certain staple items to garner new customers, *and* I am offering a drink of my fine whiskey to wet the whistle." Austin studied Fargo closely. "You don't look overly inclined to take my offer of bringing in meat for sale. I can still use a good hunter, if you want to reconsider."

"You've got Ballinger out on the road slaughtering anything that moves. Why do you need me?"

Austin looked shocked, then laughed. "You have a wit, Fargo, I'll grant you that." Austin turned sober and said coldly, "Don't let it get you in trouble." The store owner called out to another potential customer and launched into his sales pitch again. The crush of prospectors coming up pushed Fargo aside.

He watched Harry Austin for another few seconds, wondering what the man had told Ballinger to do. If the bail money had changed hands at all, Fargo knew it came from Austin's pocket. But the businessman had more important things in his pocket than money.

Like Marshal Peterson.

The prospectors rode together on their mules. The six men looked half past dead, heads drooping and shoulders slack. Fargo guessed they had come nonstop from Denver City to get a piece of the golden pie being lauded as better than the extensive strikes on the other side of the Front Range in Central City and Georgetown.

Fargo perched on the limb of a juniper, watching as they rode past. He craned his neck to see if they attracted any other attention—from Whip Ballinger. He had lain in wait for hours and had seen several groups of miners on their way to Nugget, but none had the look of easy pickings.

For all their obvious exhaustion, these prospectors were watchful and well armed. If attacked, they would fight back hard and fast. Ballinger preyed on solitary riders, shooting them in the back or from ambush.

The miners rounded a hairpin bend in the road and vanished from sight. Fargo stretched cramped muscles and knew he had to figure some other way of flushing Ballinger from his hiding place. After leaving Austin's sideshow in the center of town, Fargo had gone directly to the cabin where he had caught Ballinger before. The fireplace held only cold ashes and nothing else showed Ballinger had returned.

As he sat in the tree, waiting for what might never come, Fargo considered how to get Susanna out of her claim and recover some of the money from that sidewinder Harry Austin. Holding onto the claim for profit was a lost cause, although Susanna refused to admit it. The power of human faith was great, and she now had to prove the claim as a tribute to her dead brother. Otherwise, she would see their trip from St. Louis as a meaningless pilgrimage ending in an even more meaningless death.

Alone for another hour, Fargo shaped a plan to get money back from Austin. Bringing the man to justice might prove difficult to do since he owned Nugget and everything in it, including the marshal. But Fargo might find another way of bringing a touch of justice to the Colorado mountainside.

At sundown he finally gave up and dropped to the ground. Whistling brought his Ovaro trotting up from the grassy meadow where it had grazed all day. Fargo mounted and returned to the Grafton camp to see if Susanna would go along with his scheme. Fear lanced through him as he rode up and didn't see her.

"Susanna!" he called, thinking she might have gone up the hill to Ben's grave. "Susanna!"

"That you, Fargo?" came the weak voice from under the wagon. "She left for a spell."

"You're looking better," Fargo said, jumping to the ground and crawling under the wagon to see that Zeb had color back in his cheeks and his eyes had lost the hollow, haunted look of a high fever.

"I'll get back to whuppin' wildcats in a day or two," the young man said gamely. His grin was sickly, but he reached for water left nearby and got it to his lips without spilling much.

"Where's your sister?"

"I don't know, my fever'd just broke and I wasn't payin' too much attention."

Fargo frowned. It wasn't like Susanna to leave her brother, even if the crisis had passed.

The neighing of horses caused Fargo to scramble back from under the wagon and get to his feet.

He drew his six-shooter and hurried toward the sound when gunshots rang out.

"Git him, boys," ordered one dark figure hanging back from the other two.

Fargo made no attempt to approach quietly. The leader of the robbers heard him coming and turned. Fargo saw the foot-long orange tongue of flame licking out toward him. He shot back. The bandit's bullet missed by inches. Fargo's hit pay dirt. The robber grunted and clutched his belly.

To Fargo's surprise, a shotgun barked from behind him. The attack had been an ambush and they were coming at him from both sides. Fortunately the three men charged with coming up the rear hadn't realized Zeb was on the mend beneath the wagon. Zeb was not only feeling a little better, he was fighting off the men who had tried to sneak into the Grafton camp.

Fargo kept firing, this time targeting the men intent on Zeb Grafton. Two shots missed. A third winged the robber on his knees, trying to flush Zeb. From the startled yelp, Fargo knew he had not seriously injured the man but had alerted him to the real danger.

"Git out of here. They musta known we was comin'!" one of the remaining bandits yelled as he began a hasty retreat.

Zeb fired again at the voice. Fargo doubted the young man hit anything, but it caused the robbers to run like scalded dogs.

"We did it, Fargo," Zeb said, his voice thready. "We ran 'em off!"

Fargo heard the pounding hoofbeats recede in the night, heading toward Nugget. It wouldn't do him any good going after them because they would blend in with the crowd of miners in town.

Fargo scanned the site to survey the damage caused by the ruckus. Something didn't feel right when he heard a low whimpering and remembered. Susanna!

Skye rushed to the source of the cries and found a frightened Susanna, bound and gagged behind a tree. He pulled out his Arkansas toothpick and cut the rag tied around her head, freeing her to speak.

"What did they want, Skye?" Susanna clung to his arm after he had freed her.

"I don't know. Maybe to let you know not to leave Nugget until all debts arc paid."

"Claim jumpers, that's what they were," declared Zeb from his spot under the wagon. "They wanted to steal our gold!"

Fargo wished he had caught sight of the men so he could identify them. He hoped Zeb was right and they were nothing more than a band of crooks out to either steal supplies, or jump the Graftons' claim. Fargo felt it in his stomach and knew deep down that this had all been Harry Austin's way of reminding the Graftons just how much they owed him.

9

"You won't do anything about it?" asked Fargo. He glared at Marshal Peterson, but the lawman seemed impervious to any criticism.

"Not a whole lot I can do, Fargo," Peterson said. The weasel-faced marshal pushed back from his desk. "I got to keep the peace in town and don't have much in the way of resources to help me. I ain't the county sheriff, jist a poor ole town marshal, after all."

Fargo glanced toward the rear of the jailhouse and saw both cells were empty. This caused him to seethe, knowing how the marshal had released Whip Ballinger. For a price, any crime could be excused in Nugget—and any crime authorized by Harry Austin was ignored.

"They shot up the Grafton camp and I imagine they would have raped Susanna Grafton if they had the chance."

"Anybody actually hurt, outside of what you imagine," the marshall mocked.

"I might have winged a couple of the robbers."

"Then carryin' your lead in their worthless hides ought to be punishment enough for them rascals," Peterson said. "You want me to hang 'em for you, Fargo? It ain't gonna happen, not in my town."

From the direction of the Lucky Nugget came a round of gunshots that the marshal ignored completely.

"Claim-jumping is going to happen more and more. You'll be up to your ears in dead bodies if you don't put a stop to it now."

"Thought you said they was sending a message. Seems like they could have used the postal service for that. Now what is it, Fargo? Robbers, claim jumpers or messengers? Get your story straight 'fore you come annoyin' me the next time." Peterson squinted, thinking that he was looking tough.

"The next time, Marshal, might be a crime that will get your ass out of that chair."

"I doubt that," Peterson replied, then realized what he had said. Angrily, he shot to his feet and pointed. "Get out of my office, Fargo. Don't come back here 'less you got somethin' important to tell me!"

Fargo left. The fight at the Lucky Nugget had quieted down. The drunks shooting at each other had smashed a window but missed injuring anyone with their wild spray of lead. What attracted Fargo's attention more was the tight knot of excited prospectors in front of Austin's general store. He went to see what took them away from the wild revelry in the saloon.

"What's up there?" he asked a man at the rear of the crowd. Fargo tried to peer over the miners in front of him but couldn't.

"Assay reports. They got posted to show where all the gold's bein' taken," the prospector said.

Curious, Fargo pushed his way to the front of the crowd. A short list detailed fabulous amounts of gold turned in to Austin at the assay office and put on deposit in his new bank. Fargo's eyes worked down the list until he came to a name that turned him cold inside.

Ben and Zeb Grafton were listed as among the biggest winners in the race to extract gold. The amount they supposedly took from the river was a hundred times what Fargo knew they had found. Following this was a penciled notation that all the gold had been panned in only four days, hinting that tons more waited for hardworking miners.

He tried to tell those nearest him the list was a fraud, but no one wanted to hear. The men had come to the Front Range to find gold. To them, this proved Nugget was the center of the richest strike in all Colorado, and nothing would stop them from getting their share.

It seemed to Fargo that when one man read the list of lucky prospectors and left, two more took his place. Everyone in Nugget would soon think the Graftons were rolling in gold dust and were richer than Croesus. If the raiders the night before had in fact come after supplies, hungry, desperate, greedy men would be coming after the gold taken from the river.

Ben Grafton had already died and Zeb was injured. Susanna would never be able to support herself, take care of her brother, and fend off the buzzards that would circle because of Austin's list.

Fargo mounted his Ovaro and headed back to tell Susanna what had happened in town. If he had meant to move on, that notion was long dead.

"But we've only found less than a hundred dollars in gold," Susanna said, frowning. "Why would Mr. Austin post such a lie?"

"To sell more supplies. To get newcomers to buy the land at inflated prices. To make even more money off the ones who are already here. If you and Zeb have struck it big, they can, too." Fargo hoped that confronting Susanna with Austin's latest deception would at least force her to give up on the land.

"But we—oh, I see. I should have expected it from a man like him." Susanna's lips thinned to a line as she feared how Austin would make her erase her family's debt. As far as Fargo knew, Austin had not yet opened a whorehouse, but with hundreds of prospectors coming to Nugget every week, it was only a matter of time.

"It will be a huge loss, I know, but you should pack up the wagon and leave. Let Austin foreclose on the claim. It's little enough punishment for him, but you have to get out of here, Susanna. I'll make sure he doesn't follow you."

"He would foreclose, then sell the land for even more to someone else," Susanna said.

Fargo knew she was right. Turning tail and running

solved only part of the problem. It got Susanna and Zeb to safety, albeit in poverty, but did nothing to stop Austin's illicit scheme to milk every gullible prospector who came up the road from Denver City.

Then there was the matter of Whip Ballinger. Fargo had no doubt the killer worked for Austin, making the businessman as guilty as the henchman who pulled the trigger. One robbed on the road, discouraging prospectors from leaving without settling their balance while padding his own pocket with what he stole from those who tried. The other by using a pen and playing on greed, conning otherwise decent folk into digging themselves a hole they could never escape from.

"We will work this out," Fargo promised her. "How's Zeb doing?"

"His strength is returning fast," Susanna said, glad to change the subject. "That powder worked wonders, maybe too much. He wants to go to the river and pan for gold again."

"Set him straight," Fargo said, reading her expression. No matter what he said, her hope that wealth lay in the river still glimmered like the prize she sought out. She had too big an emotional stake. No gold meant Ben had died for nothing. No gold meant she and her brothers had risked everything they had in St. Louis pursuing a will-o'-the-wisp. She knew what a skunk Austin was, but it was hard for anyone to look back on so many bad choices and not want to make good.

"I'll be down at the river, Skye. Look after Zeb for a while, will you?"

She flashed him a quick smile, jumped to a rock so she could give Fargo a good kiss that promised much more later, then hurried off with the gold pan under her arm. The least she could do for herself was claim the seeds Austin had left behind. Fargo checked to be sure that Zeb rested easily in the shade of the wagon. The young man slept peacefully enough now that the fever had broken. His bandages needed changing, but Fargo was not going to awaken him for that chore. Rest was more important to his healing.

Fargo found himself at loose ends after he had cleaned up the camp and tended the oxen, the mule, and his horse. He was a man of action, not cut out for housekeeping, and even these chores were finished. He found himself a shady spot and lay back, wondering if he ought to go to the river and watch Susanna. For all her diminutive size, she packed in twice as much femininity as other women. Her spirit and determination—even her pigheadedness—appealed to Fargo, as well.

He was drifting off to an afternoon siesta when his Ovaro snorted and began pawing the ground. Fargo sat up, immediately alert. Whatever had spooked the horse presented danger.

Slipping his Colt from its holster, Fargo made a quick circuit of the camp. Zeb still slept, but more fitfully as if whatever spooked the Ovaro also wore on him. Fargo strained to hear anything but could not. The distant rush of the river erased all but the loudest sounds.

He stopped halfway to the river. A fresh boot print in the mud warned of unannounced visitors. He ran the rest of the way to the riverbank. Fargo looked upstream and then down, hunting for the brunette. Susanna was nowhere to be seen.

Fargo kept calm, even when he found her gold pan sitting on a rock. She might be off in the bushes and would be back soon. Then he spotted more bootprints—several different men had come here within the past few minutes. The spray from the river and the ceaseless splash of water worked to erase tracks fast.

"Susanna!" he called. "Where are you?" Fargo listened hard for any response. The wind through the tall pines and the murmur of the river were the only sounds reaching his ears. Fargo tried to find where she had worked at panning, but the spot was already eradicated by the elements. He headed upstream, following partial boot prints, but they soon vanished when they crossed rocky patches.

Fargo climbed to the top of a boulder and tried to spot the men leaving the tracks—or Susanna—but saw no one. From the condition of the tracks, the men had only a short head start on him. But what of Susanna? Had they taken her or was she off in the woods somewhere? Fargo tried to remember if she had mentioned picking berries or hunting for tubers to boil for dinner.

"Zeb," he said. Fargo jumped down from the rock and ran back to camp. Zeb was already awake and pulling himself painfully from under the wagon.

"Side got to painin' me something fierce," the young man said. Seeing Fargo's expression, he hastily asked, "What's wrong? Is it Susanna?"

"I can't find her," Fargo admitted. "There were tracks of several men down by the river, but she might not have gone with them."

"She wouldn't abandon us. She was kidnapped!"

"Get the shotgun and stay alert. Don't shoot unless you know who you're shooting at," Fargo cautioned. "I'll track them down."

"Don't let anything happen to her, Fargo. I couldn't bear it, not after losing Ben."

The edge in Zeb's voice told Fargo he would do everything possible to avenge any harm coming to Susanna, even if it meant killing.

"Keep an eye out," Fargo said, going back to the river. He searched the area again, knowing it was a futile hope that Susanna had come back on her own. He lifted her gold pan and saw a scrap of paper stuck to the underside.

Fargo pulled it off and saw the crudely lettered note. His anger surged. Susanna had been kidnapped and was being held for ransom. The price was the Graftons' claim. Fargo knew the claim was worthless and would make the exchange in an instant, but he doubted any men desperate enough to kidnap a woman would be content with only a land deed.

His hands clenched into fists, then he set out upstream to find Susanna's kidnappers.

The Trailsman kept after Susanna's kidnappers more by instinct than tracks. After less than a hundred yards, all traces vanished, but he kept moving, turning from the river when it seemed appropriate. He knew the men who had taken Susanna would be overconfident—and lazy. They thought stealing a proved claim was a better solution to their financial condition than hard work.

He picked up their trail again a half mile away from the river as they entered a wooded area. Fargo's long stride devoured the distance as he went along a game trail after them. Twilight began dulling the small signs he followed and worried him that he might have to camp for the night, leaving Susanna in their clutches. Then his sensitive nose picked up a whiff of burning pinewood from a campfire not far ahead. The scent grew stronger as he silently crept up on the camp. Three men huddled around the fire, trying to get their damp clothes dry. They had been near the river to get so wet.

Fargo circled the camp to get a better look at the men and to find what they had done with Susanna. His heart jumped into his throat when he spotted her lying unmoving near a fallen tree. Her clothes clung to her body like a second skin, as wet as any of her captors'.

"When we gonna let her no-account brother know how to sign over the claim?" asked one man.

"What's the hurry?" spoke up a second. "We can have some fun with her first. She's 'bout the best-lookin' filly in these parts."

"She's the *only* filly what don't charge," laughed the third. He shucked off his shirt, rung it out and then tossed it aside. "I reckon it's 'bout time we rode that li'l filly, too." He started to remove his pants when the other two protested.

"How come you get to go first?" whined the second man. "You always horn in. What about Sidewinder'n me?"

Fargo decided the quiet man's name must be Sidewinder. It was time to stop the argument, although he wouldn't mind seeing the three cut each other to ribbons.

"You owlhoots are at the end of your road," Fargo said, stepping from the shadows, his cocked Colt aimed at them.

The one nicknamed Sidewinder went for his gun. He had reactions matching a snake's, but Fargo was faster.

The bullet from his Colt cut through Sidewinder's heart. The man crumpled to the ground and his six-shooter fell from lifeless fingers. The other two were fumbling for their six-guns.

Bullets whined past his head, but Fargo stood his ground, methodically firing. The shirtless man was the next to die. Fargo's last bullet dispatched the third kidnapper. Only then did he notice the tiny stings on his arm and leg. Slugs had ripped through his shirt and pants, leaving shallow creases. He had come close to being gunned down, but the result of the fight left dead those who deserved it.

Fargo knelt beside Susanna. She stirred, but her eyes did not open. Gently examining her, his fingers came away bloody. He found a large knot and a shallow cut on the back of her head. He glanced at the three kidnappers and felt no need to bury them. They had kidnapped a woman, had meant to rape her, and would have probably killed her after they had the claim transferred into their names.

Kidnappers, rapists, would-be murderers, claim-jumpers, the list of their intended offenses was too big for Fargo to itemize. They had tasted frontier justice for their crimes.

Fargo got his arms under Susanna's shoulders and knees and lifted her easily. She presented no burden as he made his way back down the game trail through the forest. By the time he reached the river, Susanna stirred, moaning and trying to wiggle free. He held her tighter all the way back to camp.

"Zeb, it's me. I have Susanna with me. Don't shoot!" Fargo called. He saw the young man painfully come into the firelight from their campfire. He clung to the shotgun like a lifeline.

"Is she all right?"

"She got knocked in the head, but she'll be fine with a little rest." Fargo saw Zeb sink to the ground in exhaustion. The man's wounds were still not healed. This much worry and excitement had to take its toll on him both emotionally and physically.

"I'm glad. Thanks, Fargo."

"Get back to your bedroll. I'll tend her."

Zeb went off, mumbling as he went. Fargo saw him crawl under the wagon and fall into a heavy sleep that was almost a coma. He could only imagine the strain Zeb had been under most of the day and halfway into the night. It almost matched what Susanna had been through.

He carried her to where he had spread his bedroll and gently put her down. Fargo got some boiling water and dabbed gently at the scrape on Susanna's head. She muttered and then smiled, the tension fading from her face. Susanna held tightly to his arm, so Fargo lay beside her, staring up at the stars as she slept next to him.

10

Susanna stirred and snuggled closer to Fargo. He had been dozing but came awake. He studied the stars overhead and decided he had been asleep almost four hours. It would be dawn in another hour. Susanna sighed peacefully and started rubbing herself against him. Her legs spread enough so she could take his thigh between hers. Rocking gently back and forth caused the petite woman to purr like a contented kitten.

When her head began slipping under Fargo's shirt and working lower, under his belt, toward his crotch, he knew she was not asleep.

"You faker," he said softly. "How long have you been awake?"

"Awake? I'm dreaming. I must be because this is wonderful! And ever so hard!"

Fargo gulped as her hand circled his stiffening manhood and began moving up and down awkwardly. He reached down and unfastened his belt and got free of his pants. A sudden rush of cold night air surged around his heated length, and then he forgot all about the momentary discomfort because Susanna moved down, her lips taking him warmly.

"Umm," the lovely woman said, coming up for air. "You taste good." Before Fargo could say a word, she went back to her oral ministrations, her tongue roaming all over his sensitive column until he was rising off the ground and trying to cram himself farther into her mouth.

"Not yet," she said, licking her lips and eyeing him wickedly. Any hint of the blow she had taken to the back of her head was gone, replaced by nothing but sheer vital lust for him.

Her fingers danced lightly over his belly, around his waist, beneath his tightly muscled rump, then back to stroke just under where her lips so avidly kissed and moved up and down. Fargo felt as if her wet lips and stroking tongue had ignited a blazing forest fire in his loins. He moaned and thrashed about, in spite of trying to keep still. He didn't want the woman's mouth to leave him. And yet he did. He wanted more.

His hands stroked through Susanna's long brown hair so he could steer her in the motion he relished most. Her head bobbed faster now, but this caused Fargo's passions to rise to the breaking point when he wanted to enjoy more of what the lovely woman had to offer.

When she looked up, her ginger eyes sparkling, Fargo took the opportunity to pull her back alongside him on the blanket. Their lips met and the kiss deepened. In this position, she was able to grip his trembling stalk, and he returned some of the pleasure that she so eagerly gave him. He reached around her trim body and began working off her clothing. It was slow work, but Fargo wanted to take his time.

Every article of Susanna's clothing that was discarded let him stroke over more bare skin, to kiss the exposed white expanses, then lightly nip and caress until she was buck naked. Her firm, apple-sized breasts shone in the moonlight like silvery mounds. Fargo bent over and took one nipple into his mouth, giving it full attention. His tongue rolled the passion-hardened nub in small, stimulating circles that returned some of the joy she had already given him.

"Oh, Skye, more. I want more. Use this!" She tugged hard at the fleshy pump handle in her hand, pulling it toward the fleecy triangle between her parted thighs.

"Not yet," he said, moving to the other breast to give it still more loving care before dipping into the deep valley between the fleshy pillows. He worked his way up, kissing as he went. Susanna lifted her chin and let him kiss her throat. He slipped and slid and kissed back to an ear where he nibbled gently until Susanna turned away from him.

"The back of my neck. Kiss there, Skye. I love it so!"

He gave her what she wanted. As he kissed, he slid his hands around her trim body and moved down to stroke over the aroused woman's nether lips. She trembled now as if she had been caught out in a blizzard. One leg lifted and dropped over his hip, allowing him to press his belly against her rump and slip forward.

"Now, Skye, do it now. I want you inside me."

"Like this?" He shoved his hips forward as she guided his rock-hard manhood into her moist, beckoning crevice. Fargo grunted as he sank deeply into her interior. He was completely engulfed with new sensations now, delightful ones that made the earlier warmth in his loins seem like a dying ember in comparison.

On their sides, they moved slowly, gently, never making huge movements. This pushed both their desires to the breaking point, but Fargo was not going to rush if he could contain himself even a few seconds longer. His hand gripped one breast. He played with the mound of firm flesh by gripping the rubbery bud at the crest between thumb and forefinger. Rolling it around brought new cries of delight to Susanna's ruby lips. She shoved her butt back into the curve of his body to take him deeper into her and pressed her hand down on top of his to be sure he never left his delectable post there.

She gasped and sobbed and began moving with greater need. Fargo felt her soft flesh clamping down wetly around his hidden length as if she were milking him. Every move the woman made stimulated him more. Hardly realizing he did it, Fargo began thrusting with more force. He tried to bury himself entirely in her yearning cavity and was deep within when Susanna cried out lustily. Her body had shivered before. Now it shook as if she had been caught in a tornado.

Susanna twisted and thrashed about as she peaked. Her reaction triggered Fargo. He pulled her powerfully to him and felt his length stiffen to the point of no return. He erupted like a volcano. Together, they rolled back and forth until both of them felt like wrung-out dishrags.

Fargo relaxed his grip on her and let Susanna spin in his arms. She pressed her cheek against his chest. He felt the woman's slow, even breath on his skin.

"I am definitely dreaming," she said softly. "Reality could never be this good."

"I'm feeling a lot better," Zeb Grafton insisted. Fargo saw the young man's color was returning, but he had lost a lot of blood and the fever had taken its toll on his stamina. It might be a week or more until Zeb could get about without help.

"You take it easy," Susanna said, sounding more like his mother than his sister. "You rest. Skye and I can take care of everything until you're back on your feet."

Zeb stared at Fargo skeptically. He had never quite accepted Fargo's help as anything more than a way of horning in on the mountains of gold that had to be waiting in the river.

"I'm going into town to report your sister's kidnapping," Fargo said. "It won't do much good, but I might find out if those men had wanted posters on them."

"Marshal Peterson is more interested in reading the Denver newspaper than in arresting criminals," Susanna said tartly. Her lips thinned as she remembered the kidnapping and ransom attempt. Fargo had not told her what he had overheard the trio of kidnappers say about her. Once Zeb had signed over the claim, she would have been dead—after they had each taken a turn raping her.

"We're wasting precious time getting that gold," Zeb said.

"It's been there for years. No reason it won't be there a few days from now," Fargo said. He wanted to avoid the argument over how much gold there was to be panned. Zeb was still not likely to believe he had a worthless claim because of the emotional baggage he carried.

"Be careful, Skye," Susanna said. She hesitated to kiss him in front of her brother.

"I'll be back as soon as I can," he told her. Fargo had a long list of things to do. Finding out about Susanna's three abductors was far down toward the bottom. Whip Ballinger still strutted about the countryside and needed to be brought to justice. And behind him stood the kingpin of most of the evil in Nugget.

Fargo vowed that he would stop Harry Austin's scheme of robbing all the prospectors blind, even if it meant he could not recover the Graftons' money.

He rode slowly into Nugget and saw how big a difference only a few days had made. Men slept in the alleys between stores that had not been there the last time Fargo had been in town. A second saloon graced—or disgraced—the far end of town. This one was nothing more than a pitched tent with tattered holes in the canvas sides. Fargo figured it belonged to Austin as well, like everything else in Nugget.

Including the marshal.

Marshal Peterson sauntered along the street, puffing at a cigar and ignoring robbery and mayhem all around him because there was just too much for a single man to deal with. One man clubbed another and went through his victim's pockets. Three others fought in a triangular squabble that left them all bloody and staggering in the middle of the street. Peterson never even took notice of one man throwing down on another in front of the Lucky Nugget. Fargo started to go to the rescue of the man on the receiving end of the six-shooter but was too slow. Three others jumped the man with the leveled six-gun and knocked him to the ground.

Peterson walked past, puffing contentedly on his cigar and ignoring all the mayhem.

"You look upset, Fargo," came Austin's mocking words. The owner of the town sauntered out of the general store and struck his politician's pose, one thumb tucked in the armhole of his vest and the other hand moving in a wide arc to indicate the town. "Any reason for your sour looks when the pulse of this fine city shows it to be vital and growing?"

"Your marshal doesn't do much to maintain order," Fargo said. "Those three gents that jumped the one trying to rob the man in front of the Lucky Nugget are doing more to enforce the law."

"Them? Why, yes, they might be. Some folks in Nugget find it useful to hire bodyguards."

"Bodyguards?"

"You want to sign up for my service, Fargo? A man cannot keep vigilant all the time. No eyes in the back of your head, I know, but you won't have to worry if you hire a couple of my boys to guard your claim." Austin smiled and then his lips curled into a sneer. "Or is it still the Grafton claim?"

"Zeb Grafton is still the owner," Fargo said. "He's wondering when Ballinger will be brought to trial for backshooting his brother."

"What makes you think Ballinger had anything to do with, by all accounts, a tragic accident?"

Fargo saw Austin's expression and read the truth. Ballinger had killed Ben Grafton.

"What about the prospector Ballinger shot in the back of the head? There's no question about that crime."

"You have a knack for asking hard questions, Fargo. Judge Serviss is across the Front Range, making a circuit that might take the rest of the summer. If winter comes early, he's likely to be caught on the other side of the passes." Austin shrugged. "Mr. Ballinger might not have to answer for this heinous crime in court before next spring."

As Austin moved, he gestured grandly. His coat flapped open to reveal a curious weapon tucked into his belt at his left side. Seeing Fargo's interest, he closed the coat to hide it.

"That's a mighty peculiar-looking gun, Austin," Fargo said. "What kind is it? I thought I knew everything that shot bullets."

"A special weapon," Austin said, his fancy words leaving him now.

"Mind if I look at it?" Fargo saw Austin start to deny the request, but the man yielded. Austin lifted his coat away and drew the short-barreled weapon so Fargo could see it more clearly.

"A single-shot?" Fargo asked. When Austin turned it so the barrel was exposed, Fargo nodded in understanding. "One shotgun shell."

"It has proven useful," Austin said.

"How much gold's being found these days?" Fargo asked, changing the direction of his questions suddenly, to take Austin off guard.

"What?" Austin glanced at the shotgun-shell pistol in his hand, then shook himself as if clearing cobwebs from his head. "Plenty. More all the time. This is going to be the richest strike in history, making the American River back in '49 look puny in comparison."

"Could be," Fargo said. Austin's reaction had confirmed what he had suspected. The handmade pistol might provide serviceable protection, but it was probably used more to shoot gold dust onto rocks along the river. A shotgun shell loaded with small nuggets and dust could cover quite an area. Fargo had to hand it to Austin. It was an imaginative way of salting the riverbanks. With a few larger nuggets tossed out, such as the one Ben Grafton had found, the illusion of a huge gold strike would be built up over a few weeks.

Fargo doubted any gold not planted by Austin had been brought in.

"I have to see to my newest business," Austin said. "Buy you a drink, Fargo?" Austin pointed to the battered tent saloon. Behind it stood a dozen smaller tents. Fargo saw a tired-looking woman crawling out of one, followed by a happy-looking prospector. This would have been Susanna's fate if she had agreed to Austin's terms for erasing the Graftons' debt.

"Later," Fargo said to Harry Austin's back as the man rushed off. Fargo's keen blue eyes raked from one end of the street to the other and stopped when he saw a small group of men huddled together outside the Lucky

Nugget. He rode over and dismounted near them. They hushed as he walked up.

"What do you want, mister?" one asked suspiciously.

"You gents have the look of men fed up with what's happening in Nugget," Fargo said. He turned to watch Marshal Peterson pass by a robbery in progress.

"The louse," grumbled one prospector. "He lets thievin' like that go on in broad daylight. How are we ever gonna protect our claims?"

"A vigilante committee might be the answer," Fargo said.

"We saw you talkin' with Austin. He owns the marshal and that pack of jackals he calls deputies. Hell, he owns *everything* in Nugget," said another.

"Austin and I locked horns when I came to town a week ago," Fargo said. "A henchman of his killed Ben Grafton, and I've been riding him about that ever since."

"Whip Ballinger? Yeah, Whip takes care of all Austin's unfinished business."

"The marshal let the son of a bitch go free. Heard tell he's back to robbin' prospectors on their way between here and Denver," said another.

Fargo let their anger build as he studied them. They might be the answer to the problems in Nugget.

"What this town needs is a vigilance committee made up of honest men like you," Fargo repeated more forcefully. "If you don't take control, Ballinger and his cronies will do as they please, with Harry Austin's blessing."

"We don't known nuthin' about organizin' a vigilante group."

"What's to know? Enforce the laws of Colorado. No murder, no stealing, no claim-jumping. None of those are being enforced now, are they?"

"You mean Austin's lettin' his henchmen jump claims?"

"I can't say they worked for him, but the Graftons killed three yesterday."

Fargo let the prospectors worry about the safety of their own claims. That would lead them to worrying on other matters of greater significance.

"We need a vigilance committee," cried one. "Let's pass the word and organize tonight. Outside town at sunset."

The men cheered and went their separate ways to enlist the aid of other miners and prospectors. Fargo decided to wait around and see how the organizing went. Until then, he could ask around after Whip Ballinger.

11

"You're mighty curious about him, Fargo," the barkeep in the Lucky Nugget said, eyeing him warily. "Whip's not so bad, no matter what they say 'bout him."

Fargo wasn't going to argue. He knew how dangerous and treacherous Ballinger could be.

"So he hasn't been in?"

"Didn't say that," the bartender said. "Saw him this morning when I opened. He and Mr. Austin was talkin'. Think Whip had some important business back in Denver. He hightailed it out and haven't seen hide nor hair of him since."

Fargo knew a lie when he heard it. Whether Austin put the barkeep up to lying about Ballinger's whereabouts or if the man did it out of some misguided loyalty to Ballinger wasn't obvious. The result was the same. Fargo thanked him and drifted around the saloon, eavesdropping on some prospectors and asking after Ballinger with others. The whole time he was in the Lucky Nugget, the barkeep watched him like a hawk.

Leaving the saloon, Fargo ducked around the side and waited. He heard the back door creaking open on unoiled hinges and hurried back to see if he had flushed his quarry. His heart sank when he saw the barkeep leaving. Fargo had hoped Ballinger was hiding out and waiting for a chance to escape town. Still, Fargo thought he might learn something if he followed.

As if the barkeep was a fish on a line and Harry Austin was reeling him in, he went directly for the back door of the general store. Austin came out and listened to what the bartender had to say. Then it was Austin's turn. As the businessman talked, he grew angrier until he shoved the barkeep and sent him reeling back in the direction of the Lucky Nugget. Fargo stayed out of sight as the bartender returned to the saloon.

Fargo started to continue his hunt for information when he got the feeling he ought to wait a few minutes, since he had not overheard all Austin had to say to the bartender. Fargo didn't have long to wait. Three men showed up at the rear door and silently listened to Austin harangue them. Their heads bobbed as if they were on springs, and when they left it was with a purpose.

Fargo still had not overheard what was being said.

The trio split up and went different directions when they reached Nugget's main street. Fargo gave up on his scouting and went to the edge of town where prospectors were gathering. He listened and saw that there was a good chance for them to form a workable vigilance committee countering the marshal—and Harry Austin.

"We got our lives and our fortunes on the line," one scrawny miner said from atop a lightning-struck stump. "Crime is out of control in Nugget and out in the gold fields. Do we dare work our claims alone? Men are gettin' shot in the back. We got to worry about our throats gettin' slit."

"And they kin take our gold and the marshal don't care," piped up another. Fargo marveled at how the miners could put the cart before the horse. In spite of the ridiculous statement, this galvanized the men more than any logic could.

"We can't go running around like chickens with our heads cut off," spoke up another. "My name's Cole, Cole Robby, and I been in Nugget for only a week. It didn't take half that for me to see Harry Austin is going to eat us alive if we don't do this right the first time out."

Fargo was glad to see someone with a sense of organization taking charge. This kept him out of the picture and allowed him a free hand hunting Ballinger while the vigilantes maintained order in town.

As the vigilance committee slowly took shape, with patrols organized and rules drawn up, Fargo saw two of the men who had spoken with Austin coming from town. They said nothing to each other and split up, going to opposite sides of the crowd. He watched carefully, knowing Austin was no fool. He sent his henchmen to keep an eye on what had to be potent opposition to his iron domination of Nugget.

A more unsettling notion came to Fargo. Austin might get his men into positions of command in the vigilance committee and turn the band of prospectors into yet another source of power for himself.

"We don't need to wait for crime," piped up a shaggy-haired miner near the speaker on the stump. "That Whip Ballinger's a road agent who ambushes anyone that tries to leave Nugget without settling debts. He robbed my friend and put a bullet in his back."

"Ballinger also shot another man in the back of the head and killed him," Fargo called out. "Marshal Peterson let him out on bail. He's not only a thief, he's a backshooter and a horse thief."

"Ballinger or Peterson?" joked someone in the crowd.

"What's the difference? They're in cahoots," shouted Cole Robby. The idea of going after a road agent and killer who evaded the law sparked interest in the miners. Fargo knew part of it was a way of protecting themselves, their friends, and belongings, but another—perhaps a large part—was a way of breaking the boredom of life futilely hunting for gold.

The larger crowd began breaking up into smaller groups, all vying for the privilege of hunting down Whip Ballinger. Fargo stayed away from any particular band of men until he saw which had the best chance of bringing the outlaw to justice. Turning the vigilance committee into a lynch mob wasn't what he wanted.

"You Fargo?" asked the man who had been on the stump.

"I am," Fargo allowed. "You did a good job getting them stirred up and moving."

The man smiled crookedly. "I've been in mining camps

before and know how important it is to stop owlhoots before they get a foothold. I heard what you said about Ballinger. You have a stake in seeing him with a stretched neck?"

"Only after a fair trial," Fargo said, knowing how he walked a knife edge with these men. "Do you know where he's hiding out?"

"Not me, but a couple others saw a man answering to Ballinger's description up near Death's Bluff."

Fargo saw two men crowd close, nodding in agreement.

"We seen 'im, me and my partner," one prospector said eagerly. "Hearin' how this Ballinger's out robbin' and killin' makes us real uneasy. We lost too many friends to men like him."

"I'll see if I can find him," Fargo said. He knew where Death's Bluff was. It was rugged terrain and suited to a man hiding out.

"We all go. There's safety in numbers," the prospector said. He thrust out his hand. "My name's Jolly Dobson, and I hail from California."

"You find gold out there?" asked one of the men claiming to have seen Ballinger.

"I can scout better on my own," Fargo said, wanting to leave the men to swapping their tall tales about finding gold.

"No, we can't do that, Fargo," Dobson said firmly. "If we're going to work right, we work together. That's the reason for having a vigilance committee."

Fargo saw how other, smaller groups already had chosen their own areas to patrol and their own road agents to chase. Cole Robby seemed the most dynamic, gathering a large group around him to patrol Nugget's main street and stop the petty pilfering and gunfighting there.

"Let's go," Fargo said.

Fargo, Dobson, and the two miners reached the winding path leading to the top of Death's Bluff. One of the men stood in his stirrups and pointed to the top.

"See that? A flash of sunlight off metal."

Fargo had been watching the trail for tracks. He looked up where the man pointed but saw nothing.

"Someone rode ahead of us not an hour back," Fargo said. "The tracks are plain enough, but I can't tell if it's Ballinger or someone else."

"I tell you, we seen the varmint, Fargo. And someone's up at the top of the bluff."

"Did you see it?" Fargo asked Dobson. The man shook his head.

"We'll be easy targets if we ride together," Jolly Dobson said. "You two stay here and let me and Fargo check out the top of the bluff."

Fargo was grateful for the man convincing the other two to hang back. Riding with Dobson was dangerous enough but all four would certainly attract unwanted attention from above. If Ballinger had camped there, the result would be dangerous and possibly deadly. Even if it was someone else, he might not take kindly to four men riding up on him.

"You want to lead off?" asked Dobson. "You track a danged sight better'n I do."

Fargo said nothing as he headed up the steep path, letting his Ovaro pick its way across the loose rock. No skill was required to follow this trail. He craned his neck to see if anyone poked his head over the top of the bluff, but their advance went unseen. Glancing behind, Fargo saw Dobson intent on not slipping and falling over the increasingly steep drop-off on their left side.

"Keep going, Fargo," Dobson called as he fell back farther and farther. "I can't travel as fast as you. My horse isn't as sure-footed."

This suited Fargo. He maintained his steady pace and got to the top of the bluff less than a half hour after beginning the climb. The Ovaro nickered and shook like a wet dog when it reached the top of the trail, glad to be off the narrow path.

Not twenty feet away sat a man with his back to Fargo. A coffee pot rested in the embers of a fire and the man drank from a shiny tin cup. Fargo dismounted, dropped the Ovaro's reins and drew his Colt as he silently advanced. The man never stirred.

Fargo heard Jolly Dobson coming behind him but did not look back. He fixed his attention on the man at the fire. His heart jumped when he got closer and recognized Whip Ballinger. The man was sitting like a bird on a fence, waiting to be knocked over.

Ballinger put down his cup, stood, and turned, his hands away from his sides as if he wanted Fargo to see he was not going to reach for his six-shooter.

"You took your sweet time findin' me, Fargo," Ballinger drawled. "I'd have drowned in my own coffee if I'd had to drink any more of that swill."

Fargo caught his breath. Something wasn't right. It was as if Ballinger had been expecting him.

Ballinger moved slowly, reaching down and picking up a long oak ax handle. He held it in his right hand and lightly smacked it against his left palm.

"You're right," Ballinger said, grinning wickedly. "This is what I used to knock the brains out of Ben Grafton. What?" Ballinger laughed now. "You didn't know I was the one who bashed him in the head?" He swung the ax handle against a rock, causing a loud crack like a six-gun firing.

"Why'd you kill him?"

"You ain't as smart as I thought, Fargo. He saw Austin salting the riverbank. He would have told everybody and ruined the swindle. Couldn't have that." Ballinger cocked his head to one side. "You haven't figgered out any of it, have you? You're downright *dumb*, Fargo. Dumb!"

The instant the word left Ballinger's lips, everything fell into place for Fargo. He dropped into a crouch, cocked his Colt and spun around in time to see Jolly Dobson leveling a rifle at him.

Both men fired at the same instant. Fargo's bullet hit Dobson in the chest and staggered him; Dobson's slug knocked off Fargo's hat.

Then the heavens were split apart by lightning that blasted through Fargo's head. He fell to his knees and tried to swing his six-shooter back to plug Whip Ballinger. Through blurred eyes, Fargo saw the man towering above him with the ax handle in his hand.

The first blow Ballinger landed had stunned Fargo. The second knocked the Colt from his hand. Pain shot up from Fargo's wrist all the way to his shoulder as his arm went numb.

"You shoulda figured Austin wouldn't let you live. He was worried you knew about Grafton spottin' him while he was out saltin' the whole damned countryside. Hell, you're so stupid there isn't any reason to kill you—other than it might be fun!"

A distant swish of wood through air ended with a thud as the ax handle crashed into the side of Fargo's head. He tumbled to his side and lay in the dirt, not unconscious but barely able to do anything more than hear what Ballinger was doing.

"You stupid son of a bitch," raged Ballinger. "Why'd you let him shoot you like that?"

"You were supposed to stop him, Whip," complained Jolly Dobson. "I could have killed him anytime on the way up, but you had to be the one to finish him off. Now you went and got me shot."

"You'll live," Ballinger said callously. "I need to decide how to get the most pleasure out of putting an end to this pain in the ass."

Fargo grunted as Ballinger kicked him in the ribs. Trying to figure out what hurt most proved impossible. His wrist stung and his arm tingled, but where Ballinger's boot had landed in his ribs hurt most. Until Ballinger rolled him over and hit him on the left shoulder with the ax handle.

"Are you going to beat him to death?" Dobson asked. "Let me shoot him and get it over. We don't have all day."

"I have all the time in the world to enjoy this," Ballinger said nastily.

Fargo heard Dobson arguing with Ballinger, but the words wouldn't register. The buzz in his ears grew until it drowned out everything in the world around him. Blackness crept in at the edges of his vision, but Fargo fought unconsciousness. If he passed out now, he was dead. He had to do something to escape.

But what? Both his arms felt like lead after being beaten with the oak handle. Every breath he took sent lances of fire throughout his chest, and his legs refused to move. Ballinger had done nothing to them, but all strength had fled.

Fargo blinked hard as he tried to clear his vision. There had to be a way out of his predicament.

"All right," Ballinger shouted. "You patch yourself up. You got to explain to Austin how you let this piece of cow flop shoot you."

Fargo grunted as Ballinger began kicking and hitting him, rolling him along like a beer barrel. Fargo curled up and took the punishment on his back as he tried to regain his senses.

"All right, all right, Dobson's convinced me. Let me get you to your feet," Ballinger said. Fargo felt a strong arm circle his body. Ballinger tightened his grip and sent new pain through Fargo, but the anguish helped him take one step after another.

Then he looked down and saw that Ballinger had walked him to the edge of Death's Bluff. The edge suddenly dropped off more than three hundred feet to the canyon floor below.

"See you in hell, Fargo," Ballinger said.

Strong hands shoved him forward over the verge. Fargo fell and fell and fell.

12

Fargo learned fast why it was called Death's Bluff. He tumbled away from the dubious safety of the rocky ledge and tumbled over and over as he fell. His arms whirled about like a windmill, but he knew he could never hold any of the small bushes growing on the rocky face, even if they came within his grasp. His arms felt like logs from the punishment Whip Ballinger had meted out.

As he turned in his headlong plunge, Fargo saw the rocky ground rushing up at him. He swallowed hard, closed his eyes and then groaned when he hit. But the pain grew rather than stopping suddenly as he had expected in death. He fell more, but slower, bouncing about like tumbling dice, tree limbs raking at his face and body. Fargo bent double as his belly crashed into a limb, but he did not stay in this position for more than a few seconds. The power of his fall caused his legs to flip up and over his head, sending him downward to the ground.

He landed so hard it knocked the air from his lungs. But he was alive. He knew it because, through all the pain, he kept a picture of what he would do to Ballinger in his head. Fargo owed the road agent more than what a simple hanging would ever repay, but that would come in time. If he could lever open the trapdoor with his own hand he would.

Lungs straining, Fargo finally recovered enough to roll onto his side and wonder if he had ever felt worse in his life. He bled from a hundred tiny scratches on his face and body, but at least he could move. Slowly, painfully, he got his knees under him, took a couple of deep breaths and forced himself to stand. Dizziness hit him like a sledgehammer. The tall ponderosa pine tree that had broken his fall from the top of the bluff supported him until his vision cleared.

Looking directly up along the rough trunk, he saw the path his body had blazed through the tree. Long limbs were broken off and pine needles he had knocked free were strewn all over the forest floor. But he was alive and madder than hell.

Fargo made a more thorough inspection of his arms, legs, and body and found that he had not broken any bones. All he had lost were a few yards of skin, some blood—and his Colt. Reaching down, his fingers touched the bone handle of his Arkansas toothpick thrust into the top of his boot. The knife was all he would need to deal with Ballinger.

"Ballinger and Dobson," he said, regretting that his aim had been off when the turncoat vigilante had tried to shoot him in the back. Fargo sat to rest and recover his strength while he planned. He couldn't wait for the road agents to come down; he had to climb the trail again because they had his Ovaro.

Resting a few minutes might not have healed him, but the seething anger he tried to keep in check powered his long stride up the winding path to the top of the bluff again. He had reached the top of the trail faster than he had astride his horse, but this time stealth counted.

He fell to his belly and wiggled over the rim onto the top of the bluff, every sense alert. The small campfire still blazed, but only one man sat drinking coffee. Fargo looked around, hunting for Ballinger. The backshooter was nowhere to be seen. Jolly Dobson would do for now.

The Arkansas toothpick came easily to his hand as he inched forward. Dobson chewed on a strip of jerky, occasionally taking a sip of the steaming coffee to wash down the salty meat. He seemed oblivious to Fargo's approach until some small sound gave Fargo away.

Dobson perked up, then his hand went for his six-shooter.

"Drop it, Dobson!" cried Fargo, rising to his knees.

"Fargo! You're dead! I saw Whip throw you over the cliff!" Dobson turned around, froze for a moment at the sight of a man he thought to be dead, then aimed his six-gun directly at Fargo.

Dobson's bullet whined as Fargo tossed his knife underhand. He felt a hot sting on his cheek as the slug ripped past. Fargo waited to see if there would be a second, killing round. There wasn't.

Jolly Dobson stood with a confused look on his face. The handle of Fargo's knife protruded from the center of his chest. Dobson reached out, touched the bone handle as if he did not believe it, then keeled over. Fargo swarmed forward, scooped up Dobson's six-shooter and then pulled the knife from its bloody sheath.

Dobson didn't look quite so jolly now. He was stone dead.

Fargo wiped off the blade on Dobson's shirt, then sank down on a rock near the fire, exhausted. Slowly gathering his strength, Fargo lifted Dobson's six-gun and went exploring, only to find tracks that suggested Ballinger had ridden off about an hour ago. Fargo was glad to see his Ovaro was tied alongside Dobson's horse.

Returning to the fire, Fargo helped himself to the food and coffee, since Dobson wasn't going to be hungry or thirsty anytime soon. As he ate, Fargo considered how best to handle the growing mess in Nugget. Harry Austin held the trump cards, but Fargo knew every hand could end up a loser against a better player. By the time he finished the sorry meal, he knew what had to be done. He heaved Dobson over the back of his horse and started for town.

"You look like you rode through a tornado," marveled Cole Robby when he saw Fargo.

"Feels more like I wrestled a mountain lion and a grizzly at the same time," Fargo admitted. "But I'm still in the saddle." He jerked his thumb back to indicate Jolly Dobson's cadaver draped over his horse.

"What happened?" The question came simultaneously from a half-dozen mouths as prospectors gathered around. Fargo knew most of them had been at the vigilance committee meeting and some were probably Austin's men, as Dobson had been. It was time to sow a little discord among them and possibly win them away from Harry Austin, even if it took stretching the truth a mite.

"Ballinger's responsible. Dobson and I found him camped on top of Death's Bluff. Dobson fired, but Ballinger was quicker."

"Ballinger killed Dobson?" asked one miner in the front of the crowd. His eyes went wide in shock. Fargo pegged him as one of Austin's planted men.

"See for yourself. I fought it out with Ballinger, but he got the better of me." Fargo let some of the bitterness he felt seep out now to color his words, but everything he said was the gospel truth. It just wasn't the complete truth. "Ballinger got plumb away and there was Dobson in his camp, dead. So I brought him back for a proper burial. Does anyone know if he had a partner? Any kin?" Fargo stared straight at the miner who had turned pale at the notion that Ballinger had killed Dobson.

"I . . . I don't think he had a partner and he never mentioned relatives," the man said.

"You seem to know him better than any of the rest of us. Why don't you see to burying poor old Jolly?" Fargo handed the horse's reins to the man who shook his head and tried to back away. "Take up a collection for the burial. Jolly Dobson was a founding member of this vigilance committee, after all. He deserves recognition for all he's done for Nugget."

A cheer went up that took Fargo by surprise. Then he smiled slowly. Whatever loyalty Austin's men had as they spied on the vigilantes was eroded now. Ballinger was a mean cuss and had turned on one of their number. It was one thing backshooting prospectors or smashing in their heads with ax handles, but killing a friend had to worry even the most loyal of Austin's henchmen. Fargo hoped no one would check the body and see that Dobson had died from a knife wound rather than a bullet.

"We can't let this cayuse go gallivantin' 'round the countryside," called someone from the back of the crowd. "Fargo, you got a reputation. Can you track Ballinger?"

"I wasn't up to it," Fargo said. "Not then. And I wanted to get Dobson back among his friends, but if enough of you come with me, I can track Ballinger to the ends of the earth."

He grinned when the man holding the reins of Dobson's horse joined in as loud as the rest—and it wasn't feigned.

"I ain't nowhere as good at readin' the signs as you are, Fargo," said one vigilante, "but it surely does look like a heavy body came crashin' down from the top of Death's Bluff." The prospector stood and stared up at the body-size corridor Fargo had smashed as he fell through the limbs of the pine tree.

"You might be right," Fargo said, not wanting to start spinning tales. "But it wasn't Ballinger that came down mighty fast. He took a different trail."

"To the top of the bluff!" went up the cry. A dozen men crowded after Fargo as he led the way. There was no need for a silent approach since Ballinger was long gone and not likely to stay in the camp if he had returned and found Dobson missing. Fargo glanced back and saw the hodgepodge of men and the animals they rode. One or two of the prospectors looked fairly prosperous and rode horses. The rest were down on their luck and rode burros or balky mules.

It didn't matter to Fargo. They were united against Ballinger—and that meant against Harry Austin, too, even if most of them did not realize it.

He reached the top of the trail and quickly scanned the area around the camp. As he had thought, he saw no sign of Whip Ballinger, but he rode through the deserted camp to a rude corral. It took Fargo ten minutes of careful examination to see that Ballinger had ridden away from the verge of Death's Bluff, heading deeper into the Front Range.

"Well, Fargo? What do you say?" asked one eager vigilante.

"Tracks," Fargo replied.

"We got 'im, boys! Let's string up the murderin' bastard!"

Fargo knew better than to throw a wet blanket on their enthusiasm. Ballinger had several hours head start on them. When he had left Dobson in camp, he might have intended on returning or had been out to rendezvous with others working for Austin. He might even have intended on going to the Denver road to rob another prospector or two.

With deliberate slowness, Fargo got on Ballinger's trail. If he had galloped off, this would have fed the boisterous crowd. By taking it slow and easy, he forced them to think what they were doing even as he considered meeting up with Ballinger again. He owed the outlaw more than simple justice after learning he had murdered Ben Grafton. Fargo didn't even want to consider what he owed Ballinger personally for being thrown over the rim of the bluff.

The vigilantes wanted to lynch him, but Fargo wouldn't allow that. The law had to deal with Ballinger.

"There he is, Fargo," piped up one miner riding directly behind him. "See?"

Fargo's eyes widened in surprise. Fargo saw Ballinger heading back along the trail winding above them in the rocks. Whatever business Ballinger had must have been complete and he was returning to his camp.

"Dismount. Get on either side of the trail," Fargo ordered. He jumped off the Ovaro and pulled his Henry from the saddle sheath. Finding a good spot, Fargo looked around to be certain none of the miners jumped the gun and spooked Ballinger. To his delight, they had all expertly hidden themselves.

Whip Ballinger rode into the trap, never suspecting he was surrounded by a half-dozen angry vigilantes.

"We got the drop on you, you varmint!" cried one

prospector, rising from behind a leafy clump of jimsonweed.

"Freeze, Ballinger," ordered Fargo, knowing the outlaw wasn't going to escape. He trained his Henry rifle on the man. By this time the rest of the vigilantes had come from cover.

"Why aren't you dead, Fargo?" was all Ballinger asked.

"I wanted to stay around long enough to see you swing," Fargo said.

"Get the rope. String 'im up. There's a sturdy enough lookin' oak tree!"

Fargo fired his rifle in the air to get their attention.

"He has to stand trial for what he's done. No mob rule, no lynching."

"We knowed he done all those crimes!" protested the miner with a rope in his hands. "*You* do, too."

"He deserves to hang," Fargo said, "but it'll be done legally after a fair trial."

"In Nugget? You said Peterson let the owlhoot out of jail without so much as a fare-thee-well, and I heard tell Austin owns both him and the marshal."

Fargo had considered all this.

"I'll take him to Denver and turn him over to the federal marshal. There won't be any need to wait for the circuit judge, either. They have one or two in constant session."

"I want to hang him," grumbled a miner.

"Come with me to Denver and see him swing on the gallows," Fargo said. "But he will hang on a legally built gallows, not from some tree limb in the Front Range."

"You take him in, Fargo," spoke up another. "We got claims to work. I can't let none of them other claim-jumpers get at my stake. Besides, we have other fish to fry in Nugget. Ballinger's not the only crook and killer there."

Fargo knew they were all right. He had to take Ballinger to Denver City by himself, but it was a chore he gladly undertook.

"I'll take this," Fargo said, plucking his Colt from Ballinger's holster and returning it to his own. "Will you gents truss him up so I can get him started toward Denver?"

They all eagerly pitched in wrapping up Ballinger until he looked like a mummy.

13

"You're gonna kill me, Fargo," complained Ballinger. He tossed his head, but the rope Fargo had draped around his neck only cut into his flesh. "If my horse bolts, you'll break my neck."

"Then be sure it doesn't," Fargo said, his lake-blue eyes studying the trees along the road leading down to Denver City for an ambush. He worried that the vigilantes who had helped capture Ballinger would return to Nugget, get drunk in Austin's saloon, and then tell everyone what had happened out on Death's Bluff. It wouldn't take Austin but a few minutes to send every last one of his henchmen out to rescue Ballinger.

He tugged on the rope to be sure it was securely in place. Everything Ballinger said about the danger was true. If his horse—or Fargo's—reared, the man was likely to be strangled. This was the only way Fargo could devise to be sure he kept the slippery backshooter in custody until he turned him over to the Denver marshal.

"My neck!" cried Ballinger.

"Get used to it. This is going to be the last thing you feel before the gallows trapdoor is sprung under your feet."

"I won't swing," Ballinger boasted. "You don't know how important a man Austin is. He won't let me hang."

"That's why we're not going back to Nugget," Fargo said. They reached the fork in the road. To the left and downhill led to Denver. He ignored Ballinger's choked curses as he headed for Denver. Fargo still worried that

Austin might be more inclined to have Ballinger shot from the saddle so he couldn't testify against him. Austin was the type to cut his losses rather than risk everything he had stolen that Ballinger was not going to shoot off his mouth.

"They won't hold me, not in Denver City," Ballinger said. "I haven't done anything there."

Fargo looked at his captive. A note of panic in the outlaw's voice told him Ballinger was wanted for more than the long list of crimes he had committed in and around Nugget.

"Let's go," Fargo said, snapping the rope again. Ballinger wobbled in the saddle to keep his balance since his arms were tightly bound behind him. He was silent most of the way to Denver. Fargo wasn't sure if he didn't prefer the murderer to be bragging how he was going to get away. This lack of mouthing off hinted that he might think he was going to get off.

Fargo had not thought it was possible for Denver to be busier than it had been when he left a couple weeks earlier, but it was. Long lines of pilgrims came from the East, causing the town to burst at the seams. Both sides of Cherry Creek were built up, and now the tents stretched far to the north of Denver City.

"You better keep on ridin', Fargo," Ballinger said smugly. "You'll need eyes in the back of your head if you stay here."

"Why? You're going to be locked up and charged with murder," Fargo said. He ignored the stares of the people in the Denver streets as he made his way through the crush of wagons and pedestrians, leading Ballinger like a mad dog on a leash. He passed Bill Byers's office and considered putting the editor onto the story of what was happening in Nugget. Then Fargo decided against it. Byers was a Denver booster and not likely to publish anything in his newspaper that detracted from the image of a vibrant, growing, honest town.

"You trap that up in the hills, mister?" called a burly mountain man from the boardwalk. The man pointed at

Ballinger. "What's its pelt bring?" He laughed uproariously.

Fargo jerked on Ballinger's rope to keep him from replying. The federal marshal's office was at the end of the next block, and Fargo did not want to be distracted. He dismounted and tied up both the Ovaro and Ballinger's horse.

"I can't get down with my hands tied up. I think they're gonna fall off. Ain't felt 'em since we left Nugget. You're nothin' but a torturin' bastard, Fargo. I—"

Everything rushed in on Fargo. Here was a man who had shot a prospector in the back of the head and robbed him. He admitted to killing Ben Grafton because the prospector happened to see Harry Austin salting the riverbanks. Ballinger had tried to kill Fargo by tossing him over the edge of a tall bluff.

Fargo jerked hard on the rope. Ballinger cried out as he fell heavily and lay kicking in the dust at Fargo's feet.

"I'll kill you, I'll kill you!" he shrieked. "You can't treat me like this."

Fargo headed into the marshal's office, the rope over his shoulder. When Ballinger made no effort to get to his feet, Fargo started pulling. He was angry enough that he didn't care if Ballinger's foul head popped off. But his determination convinced his prisoner he meant business. Grumbling, Ballinger scrambled to his feet and followed, cursing as he came.

"What the hell's goin' on?" demanded a man with a battered star pinned on his vest. The lawman wore two six-shooters shoved into his belt in cross-draw fashion. Fargo had seen men who sported two six-guns because they thought it looked tough. Both handles of these six-shooters were worn from long use.

"Got a man I'm accusing of at least two murders, robbery, horse thievery, salting gold claims—you want me to go on?"

"Shut the damned door," the marshal growled. "People are starin' and I hate doin' business in front of a crowd." He pushed past Ballinger and kicked the door hard enough to latch.

"He kidnapped me, Marshal!" cried Ballinger. "He—"

Ballinger's protests were drowned out when the marshal grabbed the rope around his neck and jerked harder than Fargo ever had.

"You keep that pie hole of yours shut. I'll talk to you when I'm good and ready." He released the rope and glared at Fargo. "Those are mighty serious charges. Can you prove any of them?"

"I'm willing to testify to what Ballinger's said."

"Hearsay," snorted the marshal, perching on the edge of his battered desk. He stomped down hard on the end of the rope on the floor to silence Ballinger's outburst. "You say he did it. No witnesses? Maybe he was just bragging about it. Can't prove any crime in court."

"Are you saying I should have let the vigilantes string him up?" Fargo was outraged but realized the problems. Why should anyone believe him over Ballinger, since Ballinger was willing to lie through his teeth on the witness stand about his own guilt?

The way Ballinger smirked caused Fargo to ball his hands into fists. He forced himself to relax. Ballinger would not get away with at least two murders—and an attempt to kill Fargo.

"You'd have saved us all a passel of trouble," the marshal said. "I got more work than I can handle here in Denver City. I hired two new deputies and then caught them takin' bribes. Fired them, hired two more, and I suspect them of the same thing. There's no time for me to go out and find if what you're sayin' is true." The marshal squinted at Ballinger. "From the look of this yahoo, I'd say you're probably right, but there's no way I can collect the evidence against him."

"What evidence would you need?"

"If you're volunteering to be a deputy, I'll swear you in right now. But you won't be goin' back to Nugget. I need men on the streets here, now, day and night."

"He's a murdering thief," Fargo said.

"Don't deny it." The marshal pursed his lips, scowled, and then reached over and began shuffling through a stack of papers on his desk. "Don't get your dander up, mister. I might have a solution to all our problems."

Ballinger's eyes went wider and he tried to back away. The marshal stomped down on the rope and held Ballinger in place. The lawman whooped and held up three sheets.

"Wanted posters on him. I thought he looked familiar."

"What charges?" asked Fargo.

"Two for murder, backshooting, too." The marshal peered at the other and shook his head. "This one's for Randolf 'Whip' Ballinger. For stealing a horse. There's a reward on this one for fifty dollars."

"Fifty? That's all?" raged Ballinger. "What I done is worth more'n that!"

"You brought in a real pistol there, didn't you, mister?" the marshal said, looking at Fargo and jerking his thumb in Ballinger's direction.

"You'll hold him?"

"Of course I will. And you get yourself fifty dollars for your trouble."

"I'd rather see him hang for killing Ben Grafton," Fargo said truthfully.

"From the look of one of these warrants, there's not much chance he'll weasel out of a conviction. He upped and killed the brother of the governor over in Kansas."

"I wasn't aiming at him," Ballinger said, then clamped his mouth shut when he realized he was talking in front of a federal marshal.

"Don't matter who you were shooting at." The marshal fumbled in his lower desk drawer, took out a tin box, and counted out fifty dollars in greenbacks for Fargo. He shoved the stack of bills in Fargo's direction. "The varmint will hang, don't worry about that. I'll make sure he gets back for trial."

"He's a slippery one," Fargo warned.

The marshal hardly shrugged his shoulders, but the six-shooters miraculously appeared in his steady hands.

"I can shoot as good as I draw, too," the marshal said without a hint of bragging. "I'll see he gets to Kansas."

"Thanks, Marshal," Fargo said, tucking the reward

money into his pocket. He had the feeling the marshal was not a man to cross and one who kept his word come hell or high water, but Fargo still wished he could watch the sentence carried out. He owed it to Ben Grafton.

And to Susanna.

Ballinger fought like a trapped rat as the marshal dragged him to the cells in the back of the jailhouse. Fargo saw no reason to stay. He stepped out into Denver's busy street and immediately spotted an old friend.

"Parson!" he called, waving to the muleteer coming from a store across the street.

"Fargo, you get all that gold prospectin' nonsense out of your head? I'm startin' a regular freight run between here and Kansas City and kin use a man of your talents."

"I had an outlaw to deliver to the marshal," Fargo said.

"The one who killed the brother of your girlfriend?" Clem Parson grinned broadly when he saw how successful his needling was.

"Ballinger killed Ben," Fargo said, "but he'll hang for other crimes. I reckon that will have to be good enough."

"But not for you. Something else is eating away at you. What is it?"

"Harry Austin might not have pulled the trigger or swung the ax handle, but he's as guilty as his henchman."

"He's also gettin' mighty rich," Parson allowed. "I got a couple more wagons full of goods to deliver up in Nugget. He pays promptly."

"In gold?"

"Nope, always in greenbacks, but I've never had no trouble gettin' the local bank to honor them in gold."

Fargo chewed on his lower lip. For a man supposedly in the middle of the richest gold field in all Colorado Austin was paying only in the money he bilked out of prospectors. That did not surprise Fargo and reinforced his conviction that no one was finding gold around Nugget.

"I have to get back," Fargo said.

"To that li'l lady friend of yours?" Parson joshed. "If I had someone as purty as her waitin' for me, I might go back to Nugget, too. All I have waitin' for me up there is another bale of money, and that don't keep a man warm at night." Parson slapped Fargo on the back. "You're a good sport, Fargo. I meant it when I said you got a job—or anything else—if you ever need it."

They parted company, Parson to sell more of the freight he moved in steadily from Kansas along the trail Fargo had pioneered; the Trailsman went back to Nugget.

Fargo had serious business there with Harry Austin. And maybe some more pleasurable business with Susanna Grafton.

14

"I don't like it, Skye," Susanna Grafton said. "Ballinger ought to be tried here. Not here, I mean back down in Denver, where we can all see him brought to justice."

"I'm not happy with sending him to Kansas, either," Fargo admitted, "but the marshal seems honest enough and determined that Ballinger will hang."

"But it'll be for the wrong murder," Susanna said.

That made sense in a strange way. Ballinger's life of crime was going to end because of a murder he had committed more than a year ago, and it would never be acknowledged that he had killed Ben Grafton, but there was no way to execute him repeatedly. Fargo had to admit he would have preferred seeing him convicted of Ben's murder as well as of the unnamed prospector murdered on the road, but it was not going to happen. They had to be content that Whip Ballinger was not going to murder anyone else.

"Austin still has to answer for his crimes," Fargo said.

"I . . . I just don't know, Skye. He is always just a little removed from the crime. What he'd have in store for me if I couldn't pay back his loan ought to be against the law, but it isn't. He is an insulting, smug—"

Susanna raged on, but Fargo listened with only half an ear. There was nothing she could say about Harry Austin that he hadn't thought himself. The real problem lay in getting some money back from the flimflamming entrepreneur so Susanna and Zeb could clear their debt without ending up destitute.

"Come on down to the river, Fargo," called Zeb. "I'm going to work the stream for a spell."

"Have you found any gold?" Fargo asked. He had passed through Nugget on his way back to the Grafton claim and had made a few discreet inquiries. For all the hoopla about rich strikes, no one had brought any gold into the assay office for sale.

Zeb turned sly, looked around as if to make sure no one overheard him, then he grinned and said, "Yep. A pile of it!"

Fargo looked at Susanna, who nodded in agreement.

"He found two more nuggets, Skye. Big ones worth a hundred dollars or more."

"You still owe Austin ten times that," he said, realizing that Austin was actively salting the Grafton stretch of river again probably to stir up a new fuss over gold being recovered and keep his fake boom going.

Fargo thought Austin had all that in mind and maybe something more. He had the feeling of being in a game with a cardsharp who not only stacked the deck but changed the rules as the hand proceeded.

"I'll work with you," Fargo said. "For a while."

"Then you'll stay?" asked Susanna hopefully. She turned her ginger eyes up at him. The gleam in them told of her hopes and fears. "For a while?"

Fargo hoped that he and Zeb found enough of Austin's planted gold to put a dent in what they owed, although he doubted it. Austin salted only enough to keep their hopes high. Susanna and Zeb might believe Ballinger had murdered their brother and Susanna certainly knew what a snake in the grass Austin was, but they had no choice but to keep playing Austin's game until a solution presented itself.

He took off his gun belt and rolled up his sleeves, setting to work with the gold pan in the shallows showing the most promise. Fargo worked steadily, his mind only partially on the repetitive process. Mostly he built up the plan he had concocted to get the Graftons back their money without duping another gullible prospector.

Fargo might have worked mechanically, but his sharp

eyes caught the glint of color immediately when the slow sloshing of water carried away the dross and left a few specks of gold dust. He carefully removed the gold and put it in a small bag, then went back to panning.

An afternoon of work netted him almost a half ounce of gold.

Zeb came bounding down from his spot higher along the river.

"Look at this, Fargo. Look! We're rich!"

He held out four small nuggets. From the weight of the smallest, it must have been almost pure. Zeb had retrieved at least several hundred dollars' worth of gold. Added to the dust Fargo had panned, they had accomplished in a day what most prospectors took a week to gather.

It was too much, but neither Zeb nor his sister saw that. They were too excited over the haul and wanted to go immediately into town to pay off some of their debt to Austin.

"Hold back the gold, for a few days," Fargo urged. "Austin doesn't need it, and he hasn't demanded payment on your IOUs."

"No," Susanna said firmly. "He is a terrible man, and I will not be in debt to him one day longer than necessary. With this much gold, we can pay off as much as half of our debt."

"Not that much," Fargo murmured. Austin had salted their claim using his curious shotgun shell-firing pistol and dropping a few choice nuggets because he knew Susanna could not stand to be beholden for even a day longer than necessary.

"Even a penny less owed to him suits me just fine, Skye," Susanna said firmly.

"He wants the gold for himself. It's not yours, Fargo," cried Zeb. The young man moved better but still showed some twinges as he turned to hide the leather bag holding the gold from Fargo's sight.

"Keep your gold," Fargo said tiredly.

"He deserves some of it, Zeb," Susanna said, looking worried that Fargo might ride off. "He worked for it."

"It's our claim!"

"Keep the gold," Fargo repeated. "I'll ride with you into town to be sure you get top dollar for it."

They went into Nugget, a strained silence dampening Fargo's spirits. Zeb would never trust him, and Susanna shifted back and forth between fooling herself into thinking they could make a profit this way and understanding that Austin's scheme was designed to do just that.

Before they reached Nugget, Susanna said, "Why would he waste so much gold?" she asked. "On us, I mean? This is a fortune. Why give it away?"

"You'll see," Fargo said. He had no idea what was going to happen, but it would line Austin's pockets with even more money. The few ounces of gold dropped in the Grafton claim would be nothing more than priming a pump with a little water to bring forth a gusher.

Clem Parson had always been paid off in greenbacks, never in gold.

Fargo hung back as Zeb and Susanna went to the assay office. He saw Austin peering out the front window of his general store, watching and waiting. After a few minutes, Austin came from inside his store. A young boy rushed out behind him, bare feet pounding hard on the dirt street as he ran to the saloon.

Fargo settled down to wait out the drama.

Susanna, Zeb, and the assayer left the office and went directly to Austin's store. Rather than deal inside, Austin met them outside on the porch so Fargo could overhear—or anyone else nearby.

"What can I do for you fine folks?" Austin greeted heartily.

"Mr. Austin, this is about the richest gold I've ever seen," the assayer said.

"And you took it from your claim?" Austin asked in mock astonishment, as if he had no idea there was a speck of gold within a hundred miles. "This is a truly fine assay report," he said, hardly glancing at the chemical-stained paper handed him, as if he knew what it would say without careful study. "You folks are destined to be the richest in all Colorado!"

The boy's mission to the saloon became obvious. Dozens of prospectors came out to listen. Austin spoke just a little louder so his voice carried to the rear of the crowd.

"This bit of gold amounts to more than five hundred dollars, and Mr. Grafton and his lovely sister pulled it from their claim in just one day!"

"Five hundred?" gasped Susanna. "So much?" She looked accusingly at Fargo, as if he had intentionally undervalued their take.

"If you're applying it against your tab at my store, well, the debt's all absolved, and I'll credit you with fifty dollars, to boot."

"Our IOU is gone and you'll let us have fifty dollars more?" Zeb could not believe his ears. Neither could the onlookers. A buzz went through the crowd. This had to mean Austin saw immense potential in the Graftons' claim.

"The gold is that pure, and I want more of your business," Austin said, confirming what all but the densest of the prospectors had already figured out.

"What about the mortgage on their claim?" Fargo called out.

"Well, that is another matter," Austin said. He hurried on to extol the virtues of hard work—and the fantastic good luck riding with the Grafton family.

If Fargo had not known better, he would have thought Harry Austin was sincere. Looking around the crowd, he saw how Austin suckered the feckless prospectors into staying around Nugget and spending more of their money. Fargo had no doubt land sales would skyrocket after this public announcement of so much gold being taken from the Grafton claim in only one afternoon.

More than five hundred dollars of pure gold in one afternoon? Why, thousands upon thousands could be retrieved by harder-working, luckier prospectors.

Austin announced specials on mining equipment that were inflated by only a factor of two. The assayer hurried back to his office to record more deeds as prospectors coughed up the last of their money for choice claims higher on the river above the Graftons.

Fargo knew Austin took in ten times the value of the gold that had been salted in the Grafton claim.

"You were certainly wrong, Skye," Susanna said smugly. "Imagine wiping out our debt at the store!"

"And getting fifty dollars, to boot!" added Zeb. "That means he paid us five hundred and fifty for the gold we found!"

"He still holds the mortgage on your claim," Fargo pointed out. "What if you don't find any more gold for a week? What then?"

"We keep working," declared Zeb.

"You work until you need more supplies, which Austin will sell you at his exorbitant prices," Fargo said. "He's robbing you as surely as Ballinger did travelers on the road. Austin does it by playing on your greed."

Zeb looked confused for a moment, before mistrust eclipsed his face. "Even if Austin did plant a little gold to stir interest like you said, who's to say we didn't find our own on top of it. Besides why would he pick only our claim to salt?"

Fargo knew the reason for that. To keep him quiet. To pay him off. To pay off Susanna and Zeb for the death of their brother. If they stayed after such a calamity, there had to be gold in the claim. Austin used them as publicity for his bogus claims elsewhere. And Fargo had to admit there might be more to picking the Graftons to pieces with the illicit salting. Austin did not want to drive away the prettiest woman to be found anywhere along the Front Range.

"We're going back to camp, Skye. It's not good leaving it unguarded," Susanna said.

"I suppose," he said, distracted.

"Here," said Zeb, shoving something in Fargo's direction. Startled, Fargo took it and saw a ten-dollar bill. "It's for helpin' out on the gold pannin'. Sis is right. You should get somethin' for your work."

Fargo started to refuse, then tucked it into his pocket.

"Thanks. Why don't you both return to camp? I want to stay in Nugget a while longer."

"To drink?" Susanna said with some distaste at such

low habits. She obviously knew of Austin's brothel behind the tent saloon at the other end of town.

"I won't be too long," he promised. A shot or two of whiskey was as far from Fargo's mind as anything could be.

"Very well," Susanna said, still unhappy with him. She and Zeb climbed on their mule and rode back to camp.

Fargo sat on a rain barrel at the corner of the Lucky Nugget and watched the long line of miners in front of the land office and at Austin's store. For less than a hundred dollars' worth of gold, no matter what the assayer and Austin had said about all Zeb Grafton had brought in, Austin made a dozen times that in new sales. From what he could overhear, Austin allowed very few of the miners to carry debt with him. Cash on the barrelhead or no supplies.

Mortgages at the bank and IOUs at the store were reserved for those he wanted to keep around for future services.

Austin eventually closed his store and announced he was buying drinks for everyone who had purchased anything from him that afternoon. This brought a new cheer from the prospectors. Like the Pied Piper, Harry Austin led them to the Lucky Nugget where they would spend far more for his watered whiskey than a single round of drinks cost him.

Fargo moved to stand in deepening shadows. When the town turned entirely dark, save for the two saloons, he moved to the rear of the general store and gently tried to open the door. Barred. He stepped back, looked around and saw a different way inside.

He moved the empty water barrel where he had sat earlier to the edge of the store, climbed on it, and then hoisted himself to the roof. Fargo made his way to the rear of the store where he had spotted a few loose boards. Prying them up, he made an opening large enough to shimmy through. He hung by his fingers a moment, then dropped lightly to the wood floor. The echo of his boots hitting the floor rang out like a gunshot, but there was no one but Fargo around to hear it. Everyone else was drinking at the Lucky Nugget.

Fargo ignored the front of the store and concentrated on the rear section until he found a cabinet with a sturdy lock on it. Austin was not the sort of man to keep money overnight in his store. He would either carry it with him or put it into the newly arrived safe at his bank, but Austin had not had time to transfer it between closing the store and leading his band of gullible prospectors to the Lucky Nugget for a round or two of whiskey. Fargo ran his fingers around the cabinet until he found a weak spot.

Bending the flimsy side of the cabinet out, he reached inside and pawed around blindly until he found several bulging leather bags of gold dust. Fargo left them but pulled out the peculiar pistol he had seen tucked into Austin's waistband to examine it carefully. It gleamed a bright gold around the muzzle, proving that Austin had used it for salting gold dust.

Two more lumpy bags revealed nuggets like the ones Zeb had discovered. Using his Arkansas toothpick, Fargo cut small X's on them before returning them to the cabinet. He hefted the bags of gold dust but saw no way he could mark the contents. He checked the chamber of the pistol and found a shotgun shell charged with almost a half ounce of gold dust. He returned this to the cabinet, also.

Fargo had use for the gold, but there was so little of it Austin would notice right away if any of it turned up missing. For what Fargo planned, he needed another source of gold. And he knew where to get it.

He retreated through the hole in the roof, put the planks back as well as he could, then returned to the Grafton camp, forsaking the lure of a free drink at the Lucky Nugget. Somehow, he wasn't in the mood to drink Harry Austin's liquor.

15

Fargo slipped into camp after midnight, but he was not surprised to see Susanna sitting up and waiting for him. She had the shotgun nearby but made no move for it when she recognized him.

"Well?" she asked sarcastically. "Did you have fun in town?"

"It wasn't like that," Fargo said. Her brother slept fitfully under the wagon. Zeb had made progress healing from his wound, but he still showed signs of weakness. The way he snored told Fargo nothing short of a cattle stampede would wake him, but he still felt uneasy so near him. "Let's walk."

"You need to work off the drunk?" Susanna sniffed but caught no hint of liquor. Fargo couldn't tell if this made her angrier.

Susanna walked a few feet from him as they made their way down to the river. Fargo doubted Austin would be out salting tonight because of the blowout still going on in Nugget. The man had little need of adding more fuel to the fire he had built. The prospectors would be flocking out to find their fortunes—while leaving behind all their money at Austin's general store or his saloons.

"Zeb still thinks I'm trying to steal your claim," Fargo said. "Do you think the same?"

"No," Susanna said. "You're not like that, but he doesn't trust you the way I do."

Fargo tried not to laugh at that. Susanna was irritated that he had taken a few hours returning from town and thought he was out drinking and whoring. Nothing could have been further from the truth.

"I want what's best for you and Zeb, but I can't go straight for it," he said. "If I build a fire under the federal marshal and Austin is arrested, you are out all the money you paid for this claim. You're about even on supplies."

"The expensive supplies," Susanna said. She moved a little closer. Fargo helped her climb a slippery rock. Together they sat atop it, looking down into a tranquil pond away from the rush of the river. The waning moon rose over the pines and sent silvery arrows glancing off the gentle ripples in the water.

"I found proof in Austin's store that he has been salting the river. Ben saw him, and that's why Ballinger killed him."

"Zeb isn't so sure now," Susanna said.

"Are you?"

Susanna did not answer. She reached up and played with a lock of her hair, alternately looking out of the corner of her eye at Fargo and at the shallow pond.

"Austin has to pay for everything he's done to bilk prospectors, but if he is sent to prison, no one gets any money. I have a few ideas how to get your money back."

"I have a few ideas myself," Susanna said. She began unbuttoning her blouse and tossed it aside. Naked to the waist, she seemed to be cast in liquid, flowing silver in the moonlight. The lovely brunette lay back and wiggled off her skirt and frilly undergarments. She kicked free of her shoes and stood on the rock buck naked.

Fargo had watched silently as she stripped off her clothing. Susanna wasn't too tall. He reached up and cupped her bare breasts. Susanna moved closer, reaching up to press her hands on the backs of Fargo's. She shivered, and he did not think it was from the soft wind blowing off the river.

"Your hands sure do work wonders," the diminutive woman said, moving even closer to him. His face was level with the fleecy region nestled between her thighs. Burrowing down, he kissed and licked at her nether lips and turned her wobbly in the knees. Susanna slowly sank down, Fargo following. His tongue entered her and then slipped out, moving up across her heaving belly, to her deep navel and upward to play with the cherry-hard nubs atop each of her breasts.

"I feel so weak," she said softly. "Weak and excited because of you, Skye!"

She pulled him to her, kissing him hard. Her questing fingers began stripping off his clothing and soon Fargo was as naked as the woman under him.

"That can't be comfortable stretched out on the rock," he told her.

"You can make me feel a lot better," she said, grinning wickedly as she grabbed for his erect manhood. Her fingers curled around his shaft and tugged him toward the spot where he had begun kissing her body, but Fargo resisted.

"What's wrong?" Susanna demanded. "You're not worn out from last time, are you?"

"I told you what I did in town."

"Oh yes, breaking and entering," she said, her humor returning. "There's no need to break anything here. Just enter!"

Fargo's arms circled her trim, firm body. With an easy surge, he picked her up and then jumped. Susanna cried out in surprise. Then she gasped when they hit the cold water together. The pool was only waist-deep, but they had been drenched. Fargo touched her rock-hard nipples and tweaked them, rolling the rubbery tips between his thumbs and forefingers until Susanna was moaning with desire for him.

"The cold water has a different effect on you," she said. She rubbed her palm over his crotch. The sudden immersion had robbed him of his iron length, but Susanna refused to stop until Fargo again filled the circle of her warm hand.

He held her close, kissing her deeply. Their bodies pressed together as the water gently lapped around them. For Fargo it was just under his waist. For Susanna, the water came up over her belly, hiding the lovely brunette's most exciting region.

His hands began moving away from her taut nipples and the firm breasts under them. Stroking over the woman's back caused her breath to come in short, quick gasps. When he gripped her trembling buttocks, Susanna lifted one leg and wrapped it around his waist. This pressed their crotches firmly together.

She began rocking up and down, rubbing her most intimate regions against his hip. His fingers tightened on her rump and lifted. Susanna hopped out of the water and wrapped her other leg around his waist so she could lock her ankles behind his back.

Fargo staggered slightly on the slippery rocks, then got his balance. He gazed into Susanna's ginger-colored eyes. In the moonlight they took on gold highlights, as if he was staring into the beginning of the mother lode.

"Do it, Skye. Now. I want you so!"

He bounced her up and down, helped by the gentle movement of the water in the pool. When he lifted her hips enough to position her properly, they both knew it. Susanna sank down and took him fully into her gripping, heated interior.

"Oh, Skye," she sobbed out. "You're so big in me."

The sudden intrusion into the clinging sheath that so completely clutched at his hidden column robbed Fargo of words. He leaned back a little and drove another inch deeper into the woman's yearning interior. As Susanna leaned back also, the two were joined as fully as possible.

Using the water to support both of them, Fargo rocked to and fro so his fleshy pillar moved slightly within her warm, moist crevice. Fargo blinked water from his eyes and saw Susanna arching her back. Her hair floated gently on the water, her breasts were proud and firm and delectable and the look of stark joy on her face spurred Fargo on.

He began pumping with his hips, causing waves to go from one side of the shallow pool to the other. As the water churned, so did their emotions. Every movement of his hips caused him to slide in and out of her tight cavern. Susanna moaned and sobbed and began twitching. Her fingers tightened like steel bands on his upper arms.

Fargo slipped farther from the woman's delightful inner warmth and found himself surrounded by cold water. But he wasted no time and the water did not rob him of his steel. He immediately thrust back, grinding his groin into Susanna's.

Their passions ebbed and flowed, mixed and built until neither could hold back. Susanna cried out in desire as her entire body shuddered. Her enthusiastic release caused Fargo to lose his balance. He clung to her as he went underwater. Pulling her firmly to his chest, Fargo rolled over and over in the water until he got his feet under him again. Sputtering, they both came out of the water, their desires increasing with every stroke, move, and twist.

A tide built within Fargo's loins. When Susanna clutched at all parts of his body in a new release, Fargo could no longer control himself. The volcano within erupted. He tried to split her apart with each thrust. She took every one and gave back as good as she got.

Fargo made one last convulsive drive, then sank down to his knees on the bottom of the pool. Susanna splashed around and collapsed beside him. The water came to her chin. Fargo slid down to sit on the bottom so their faces were both barely out of the water.

"A bath and more," she said, staring into his eyes.

"How much more?" he asked.

She showed him.

Fargo hung around the claim, as much for what he and Susanna did at night as to build up the illusion of working the claim with Zeb. Zeb panned and worried and risked life and limb in his hunt for more gold, which never quite turned up. Fargo set about stacking worthless rocks near the wagon and then covering the pile with a canvas tarp. After a week, he was ready. He hoped Susanna wouldn't change her mind about going along with his charade.

"Hurry back," she said longingly. Susanna stood on

tiptoe and kissed him passionately, much to her brother's disgust. If there was a weak link in the chain Fargo forged, it was Zeb Grafton.

"I'll be back before you know it," he told her. She kissed him again and then Fargo set out for Denver City.

The wagon was overflowing with supplies. Fargo snapped the reins and kept the mules moving until he reached a spot just past Austin's general store. He made a big show of wiping the sweat from his forehead as he looked around Nugget. He had been gone for almost a week and hoped Zeb had continued working the claim as hard as he had been earlier.

"What's in the wagon, Fargo?" asked one of the men who had helped the vigilance committee.

"More equipment for the claim," he said, jumping down.

"Where'd you get it? Denver?"

"There's not this much mining equipment in Nugget, that's for sure," Fargo said, wiping more sweat from his forehead.

"Why do you need so much?" More men he recognized as having ridden with him after Whip Ballinger gathered.

"You daft?" cried another man, hitting him on the shoulder. "Don't you know why? Because Fargo's hit it big. Ain't that right, Fargo?"

"Depends on what you call big," Fargo said. "Come on into the Lucky Nugget. I'll buy you a round of drinks. Everyone!"

A whoop rose and a small crowd flocked after Fargo into the saloon. The barkeep smiled and waved to him.

"Haven't seen you in a spell," he said. "You want a beer?"

"A bottle of that special whiskey Mr. Austin keeps under the bar," Fargo said.

"You can't afford . . ." The bartender's voice trailed off when he saw the thick wad of greenbacks Fargo pulled from his pocket. It was big enough to choke a cow.

"The good stuff. For everyone," Fargo said, dropping

a pile of bills on the beer-stained bar. A new cheer went up, and everyone tried to get near Fargo to slap him on the back and remind him they had been part of the vigilance committee and his best friend ever.

The drinking went on until Fargo took one miner aside and said in what seemed a conspiratorial fashion but was loud enough for a dozen nearby revellers to overhear, "You own the patch of river just above the Grafton claim, don't you?"

"Well, not exactly, Fargo. About a mile upstream."

"What's it worth to you to sell?"

"Sell?" The miner seemed confused by the offer.

"How much do you want for your claim?"

"Are you buyin', Fargo?" chimed in another miner.

"Could be. You own a few feet of river downstream from the Graftons, don't you? I'd be willing to dicker for your claim, too."

As he talked loudly of buying up claims along the river, Fargo saw the barefoot boy who worked for Austin peering through the door of the Lucky Nugget. The boy lit out when he noticed Fargo's eyes on him. Fargo stirred the pot a bit more, bought another round, then left the Lucky Nugget and went to the tent saloon where he repeated offers to buy claims.

A rousing good party was going on when Fargo exited the tent saloon and started for Austin's store. He saw the man poking about under the canvas tossed over the merchandise in the back of the wagon.

"Something I can do for you, Austin?" Fargo asked. Harry Austin jumped like a boy caught with his hand in the cookie jar.

"You've got a powerful lot of equipment, Fargo. Is it all for the Grafton claim or are you going into competition with me and starting your own store?"

"I'd never compete with you, Austin," he said, tugging the canvas back into place. "Truth is, I want to settle accounts."

"What accounts?"

"The Grafton account."

"They have a credit at my store. Fifty dollars. They

brought in some mighty fine-looking nuggets, you remember."

"I meant the mortgage on their claim your bank holds."

"That's purty near a thousand dollars," Austin said, his eyes narrowing. "How do you intend to pay off such a large amount?"

Fargo pulled the thick wad of greenbacks from his pocket and started peeling off large denomination bills, then he stopped, chewed thoughtfully at his lower lip, then tucked the poke back into his pocket.

"I think the usual way of handling such debt is to ask for a discount for payment in full if it's paid in cash."

"In full?"

Fargo shrugged. "Why not?"

"Where'd you get all the money?" Austin asked bluntly. "And the wagon. That's a brand-new wagon."

"The equipment in the bed's new, too," Fargo pointed out.

"But—" Austin started.

"I need to get to camp so I can set up the equipment. Do you mind?" Fargo pushed past Harry Austin, climbed into the driver's box, and took the reins. He stood, moved the thick roll of greenbacks in his pocket so it wouldn't rub him wrong, then sat again and got the mules pulling.

Fargo forced himself not to look back as he drove out of Nugget. But he didn't have to look to know Austin stood in the middle of the street staring at him in disbelief.

16

"Where did you get all this, Skye?" Susanna stared at the wagon loaded so full with equipment that its axles creaked as he made his way through their symbolic gateposts and up the rutted path to the Grafton camp.

"Don't worry about that," Fargo said. "I have some bags in the back. Can you help me get them out?" Fargo jumped to the ground and went around to lower the tailgate. He hefted one of the four burlap bags up on his shoulder and staggered off. He had not realized they would be this heavy since he had not loaded them in Denver.

"I can't manage this," Susanna said. "Should I get Zeb to help?"

"Let him keep panning down at the river," Fargo said, dropping his bag some distance from camp. "Why don't you start filling these empty burlap bags with some rocks?"

As Fargo carried the other three bags, Susanna scrabbled in the ground and got a shallow trench dug. He added his strength to digging in the hard ground while she filled the empty bags. Fargo lugged these to the mound he had built up almost two weeks earlier, making the heap into a mountain. He positioned the sacks he had brought from Denver strategically and finished the chore with a tarp thrown over the pile.

"This is pretty obvious, Skye," Susanna said after walking around and eyeing their handiwork. "Don't you think we ought to hide it better?"

"Hide it, maybe, but not better." Fargo yanked some stubborn greasewood shrubs out by their roots and dropped them on the cache. "That'll do it. We don't want to make Austin hunt too much."

"I don't know why you're doing all this, Skye, but I hope I know the reason." Susanna came closer, her hands resting warmly on his chest. She looked up at him with her beautiful ginger eyes. He started to kiss her when he heard a commotion back in camp.

"Zeb," she said in disgust. "He finished early today."

"I want to be sure he plays his role," Fargo said. He was enjoying the notion of getting back at Austin, even if the worst of the man's crimes would probably go unpunished. Stripping the businessman of all his money might be punishment enough, but Fargo wanted to see Austin on the gallows alongside his henchman.

Susanna and Fargo returned to the camp, brushing dirt off their hands. Zeb hardly noticed because he lay down, eyes closed. He looked peaked and drawn but was unlikely to stop panning.

"Are you all right?" asked Fargo.

"Tired. I need to pace myself better. I got excited when I found a patch that looked promising." Zeb sagged a little more. "I didn't find anything."

"You will," Fargo said. Susanna looked at him but said nothing as she went about fixing the evening meal while Fargo went down to the river to complete his preparations.

After they ate, Zeb crawled into his bedroll and fell asleep almost immediately. His sister stared at him, tears in her eyes.

"It's killing him," she said. "He won't quit."

"Mining for gold is hard work," Fargo agreed. "If my plan works, Zeb won't have to do it much longer."

"You are—" Susanna started but Fargo held up his hand to silence her. His Ovaro had whinnied. Something came to their camp. It might be a wolf or coyote prowling in the night, but Fargo doubted it walked on four legs. More likely, the predator came on two.

"What do you hear?" Susanna whispered.

"I think we're getting a nibble," he said. Fargo considered staying in camp with Susanna, but he wanted to be certain the bait was taken. He motioned for the brunette to stay put, then he faded into shadows and drifted into the night as silently as any breeze blowing across the rocky land. Fargo moved to the river and waited a few minutes for any unnatural movement.

A fish jumped out of the river, intent on a night-flying bug. The restless waves lapped against the rocks along the shore as it carried all too few grains of gold down from higher elevations. And a shadow shifted within a shadow where there should have been no movement. Fargo flattened himself on a broad wet boulder as Harry Austin moved down the riverbank, clutching his salting gun in one hand and a six-shooter in the other.

Fargo waited to be certain the man was alone before slipping away and circling to the spot where he and Susanna had buried the bags of rocks earlier. He had scouted the perfect observation point and wedged himself into the niche in a rocky face of a cliff above the spot to wait impatiently.

Less than ten minutes later the trail he had planted from the river felt new boots on it. Fargo smiled when he saw Austin carefully following the track, occasionally dropping to one knee to pick up a speck of rock and tuck it into his pocket.

Austin almost fell over the mound Susanna and Fargo had made. The man tucked his pistols into his pockets and ripped back the tarp to find the burlap bags stuffed with rocks. Fargo sucked in his breath. He worried Austin might burrow down to the bottom layer of bags, but the man worked as if Fargo had told him what to do. Austin pulled out a knife and slit open the top bag.

The crooked businessman fumbled about and pulled out a handful of rock. Austin held up the pay dirt and let it run through his fingers. Even from several yards away, Fargo saw the gold flecks glinting in it. Austin was fascinated by the golden cascade and repeated it several times. Then he hastily stuffed a few of the larger nuggets from the bag into his pockets and tried to close up the cut the best he could.

Austin pulled the tarp back over the mountain of bagged rocks and worked as hard as Fargo had at replacing the shrubs hiding it. Then he retreated, vanishing in the night in the direction of the river. Fargo waited almost twenty minutes to be certain Austin was gone before wiggling from his hiding place.

Everything was going as he had planned.

"He's on his way," Fargo called. "Is Zeb down at the river?"

Susanna hurried to a spot a few yards away where she could look down at her brother. She waved the all clear. Fargo knelt beside the fire where he heated a beaker filled with colored liquid. The odor was enough to make his nose wrinkle. All the better.

Fargo looked up as Harry Austin rode into camp.

"Top of the morning to you," he greeted.

"What brings you out here?" Fargo asked, a note of suspicion coming into his voice. He put down the beaker of liquid and moved to hide what he was doing. Small nuggets were strewn all around where he had been working. Austin's sharp eyes caught both the bubbling blue liquid and the glint in the rocks.

"I've been thinking on how unsporting I was with your brother, Miss Grafton. I am a fair man. If you feel you have been cheated, I am prepared to make an offer for this claim."

"The entire claim?" asked Fargo.

"That's an odd question," Austin said, frowning. "Why wouldn't I want it all?"

"Oh, nothing," Fargo said, feigning indifference. "I thought you might want only the few hundred yards around this camp."

"What Mr. Fargo means is that I would gladly get my brother to sell the part of our claim upstream from this point."

"Where is Zeb? Hard at work?"

Austin saw the equipment Fargo had brought from

Denver in various stages of assembly around the camp. There was enough machinery to keep a dozen miners busy.

"Of course. He feels an obligation to his deceased brother to work harder than ever," Susanna said. She wiped her hands, looked disapprovingly at Fargo and his noxious experiments, and went to Austin. "Are you willing to make an offer?"

"Five hundred dollars for the entire claim," Austin said, as if this made him king of the charitable men in Colorado.

Susanna paused in surprise, then laughed wholeheartedly. "You are joking, sir. That's nowhere near the amount we borrowed from your bank."

Austin shrugged and replied, "Profits need to be made. I think it is quite generous."

Fargo deposited a blue drop of his liquid on a rock, then tossed the stone over his shoulder.

"Five hundred for the top quarter of the claim," Fargo said. "That'd be fair."

"What of the rest?" Austin couldn't keep his eyes off the extensive equipment set up around the camp.

Fargo shook his head and looked hard at Susanna. She smiled sweetly and held out her hands, as if she was a prisoner of circumstance.

"I'm sorry. There's no way we can ever agree to selling that."

"I may have to foreclose on your mortgage," Austin threatened. He stepped back, his hand going for the six-shooter at his belt when Fargo rose, towering over him.

"Do you want me to pay him off?" Fargo asked, pulling out his thick roll of greenbacks.

"Paper money, or is there a discount for gold dust?" Susanna asked, the smile never leaving her lips.

"I, uh, there's likely to be a service charge. A termination fee."

"It doesn't matter," Fargo said. "Any amount. It'd be worth it to get you out of our hair."

"One thousand dollars!" blurted Austin. "I'll offer you one thousand for the entire claim!"

Susanna started to speak, but Fargo cut her off.
"We'd rather pay what's due your bank," he said.
"I can't go any higher," Austin sputtered.
"Then don't," Susanna said. "We're happy retiring our debt and working *our* claim."
Austin started to say something, then realized he would regret it with Fargo standing so close. The businessman clamped his mouth shut, mounted, and rode away.
"See you in town, Mr. Austin!" Susanna called after him as she gave him a cheery wave.
"See you in hell," muttered Fargo, but he had to smile, too. Everything was working out just fine.

"You'll be safe if you stay in camp," Fargo assured her. Susanna clung to him, her face pressed against his chest.
"This seemed like a good idea when you suggested it, Skye. I'm not so sure now."
"Three vigilantes will keep guard around camp to protect you and Zeb. Zeb won't even know they're here."
"Do you trust them?"
"These three, yes," he said. Fargo had spent the better part of the afternoon talking with Cole Robby and a half-dozen other vigilantes. They had grown increasingly worried about claim-jumpers when a prospector a few miles up along the river had been murdered the day before. Cole and a handpicked group without ties to Harry Austin were determined to bring justice to Nugget.
"You ready to go to town, Fargo?" Cole asked in a gravelly voice.
"I'll ride ahead. Has the word been spread?"
"Two of the boys spent an hour shootin' off their mouths 'bout how you struck it rich here and was takin' the gold back to Denver for safekeeping tonight."
"That should set the hook," Fargo said. Susanna caught his arm, looking worried, then let him go. He wanted to kiss her, but it wouldn't be right in front of Cole and the other vigilantes. Fargo mounted his Ovaro, settled the heavy saddlebags and set off. As he rode into

the darkness, he checked his Colt. He had already made certain his Henry carried a full magazine.

He was as ready as he would ever be.

Fargo just didn't expect the ambush to happen so fast or the way it did.

"Hey, Fargo," came a familiar voice when he had been riding for less than fifteen minutes, heading for the Denver City road. "Wait up." Marshal Peterson stepped from behind a pine tree.

"Marshal, what can I do for you?"

"Well, sir, it's like this. I figger you got a couple thousand dollars' worth of gold in them saddlebags and I want it!" The lawman whipped out his six-gun and pointed it straight at Fargo.

"Tired of being Austin's lapdog? Think you can make a few dollars by being a road agent?" asked Fargo.

"He's not double-crossing anybody," came another voice he recognized. From the shadows to his right came one of the men who had ridden with Jolly Dobson, his rifle leveled with Fargo in the sights.

"So Austin knows you're here? Why didn't you just shoot me in the back of the head like Ballinger always did?"

"Austin wants to know how much gold you got and where you're getting it."

"Not from the part of the river he salted," Fargo said.

"Get down, slow-like. If you won't tell then we'll pry it out of you. That's gonna be a whole lot of fun," Peterson said.

"It won't be that easy, Marshal," Fargo said.

"I'd as soon cut you down where you sit, Fargo," Peterson snapped. "Austin's got other plans for you. He wants to know how rich that strike at the Grafton claim is and—"

Fargo didn't know what alerted the road agent, but Peterson swung about, his rifle dropping from Fargo to a spot down the road. Never hesitating an instant, Fargo went for his Colt and got off a shot that staggered the marshal. Fargo was not sure if he had winged him, but it ruined Peterson's aim enough to let Cole and another vigilante gallop up.

Fargo swung around, his six-shooter trained on the man who had ridden with Dobson.

"Good going, boys," called Peterson, struggling to stand straight. "I tried to get the drop on him, but—"

"Shut up," Fargo said coldly. "The Nugget Vigilance Committee members have heard everything you've said and seen what you've done. You're as guilty as Dobson and Whip Ballinger of murder and robbery."

"No, not me," shouted Peterson, throwing up his hands when he saw he could not bluff his way out of this fix. "Austin done it. He's responsible for everything. I'll testify to that!"

"Cole? You and the other boys want to get these two coyotes to the Denver lockup?"

"My pleasure, Fargo," said Cole. He securely tied up both of Austin's henchmen and headed toward distant Denver and the federal marshal's office.

Fargo watched them fade into the night, Peterson already yammering about everything illegal Austin had done. He checked his saddlebags, turned the Ovaro, and headed for the river. He had plenty of work ahead of him before sunrise and wanted to get started on it.

17

"Yessiree, that'll pay off my IOUs," the miner said cheerily, shoving a small leather sack across the counter to Harry Austin.

"Been real good out in the claim, eh?" the businessman said, laughing. His eyes widened when he opened the bag and a dozen small nuggets tumbled out. "Why, there's more'n a hundred dollars' worth of gold here!"

"I make it higher than that. I did a bit of assayin' on it myself. You can't go dupin' me about it no more, Mr. Austin. I kin make a danged sight more than two hundred dollars by takin' the whole pouch to Denver City."

"I—don't do that," Austin said hurriedly. "This gold came from the river? All of it?"

"I was standin' on the riverbank mindin' my business and suddenly there it was, gleamin' up at me. A goddamn miracle," the miner said enthusiastically. "A golden miracle!"

Fargo ducked from the general store to keep from laughing out loud. Everything the prospector said was true, but he had left out a few items. He had been on the shore when he spotted the gold, but Fargo had handed it to him after convincing him the small hunk of gold he had already collected that day was the result of Austin's salting. The small cross Fargo had cut in the nuggets from Austin's cabinet earlier had sealed the identification.

A handful of nuggets added from Fargo's stash and the charade was ready. The miner played his part to perfection. Fargo waited in the shade of the porch at the Lucky Nugget across the street until the miner came hurrying out, flipping through the greenbacks he had gained selling the gold to Austin.

"Jist as you said, Fargo," the miner declared. "He tried to buy my claim, but I tole him no!"

"Don't get too greedy. Hold out for enough to cover your expenses."

"Don't know what to do," the prospector said. "I break even. So what?"

"So you'll have a grubstake to find a real strike somewhere else, one that at least gives you a fair chance at getting rich."

"And not line the pocket of an egg-sucking dog like Harry Austin," the miner finished, flashing an even bigger lopsided grin. He looked at the greenbacks longingly, then at Fargo. "You said I had to give you the money I got from him."

"Keep twenty," Fargo said, taking the rest. The miner knew his metal and had forced Austin to pay the going rate in Denver. That made up for the twenty Fargo let the man keep for his trouble. "And don't take more than's fair for your claim."

"He came mighty close," the miner said wistfully. "I was weakenin' and he knowed it."

"Austin will up the ante. He won't be able to help himself." Fargo smiled as he thought of the greed that gnawed at Austin's gut. The businessman saw nothing wrong in gypping the avid, earnest prospectors coming to Nugget, so it was only fair to hit him where it would hurt the most.

He deserved everything he would get. Fargo hoped it would be enough to satisfy his own personal need for justice.

Fargo made his way to Austin's bank and went in. While waiting in line in front of the teller nearest Austin's broad oak desk, he judged angles, distances, windows, and what it would take to finish his part of the scam. He got to the teller and asked to change a twenty-dollar greenback into a gold double eagle.

"We don't do exchanges that way," the teller said, irritated. "Give me the double eagle and I'll be more than happy to give you paper money."

"Well—oh, the bill got away from me!" Fargo's twenty fluttered across the counter and to the floor at the teller's feet.

When the teller bent to retrieve the bill, Fargo placed a mirror he had brought with him on Austin's desk. He hastily positioned it using a ledger book as support and then waited for the teller to shove the greenback at him and silently urge him to clear out of the bank.

Fargo was more than happy to go. He doubted Austin would be in the bank the rest of the day because of the action at the general store and would not notice the mirror had been added to the clutter on his desk.

A steady line of miners went into Austin's store to pay off their debts. The last one out spotted Fargo and came to him, almost running. His grin split his face almost from ear to ear, showing blackened teeth and gaps.

"He done it, Fargo. You said he would and he did."

"Austin bought your claim?"

"For twice what I paid."

Fargo did some quick calculations and nodded. "I've heard tell of a big gold strike on the other side of the Front Range, near Georgetown."

"Me, too. Thanks, Fargo. I owe you. If we ever cross paths again, I'll buy you a drink. Hell, I'll buy you the whole danged saloon 'cause I'm gonna strike it rich!"

Fargo slapped the miner on the shoulder and got the man on his way. He had about broken even after paying exorbitant rates for his supplies and having to agree to the high rates at Austin's bank to finance buying his worthless claim. Fargo wanted to see more of the men selling out in the same way. Austin had to be feeling uneasy now that he believed land that he had salted brimmed with real deposits of gold.

And that he had let it slip out of his grip because he thought it held nothing but worthless rock and river.

The Lucky Nugget had never been crammed so full. Fargo stayed outside, finally meandering down the street to the tent saloon around sundown. The sides of the battered tent had been rolled up to make room for the crowd here, too. If Austin had played it straight, he could have made a fortune legally. Fargo prowled the edge of the crowd of drunken miners looking for Austin. He spotted the man getting a miner drunk whose claim butted up against the Graftons'. Watching for a few minutes assured Fargo the miner was not so drunk he would tell Austin where the sack of gold dust on the table had come from.

Austin finally tucked the bag into his pocket, then pulled out a piece of paper. The miner signed and received a stack of greenbacks in return.

Another prospector free of debt and able to move on to more golden shores.

Fargo dogged Austin as he moved around, buying up claims he had once ardently sold. One or two of the miners were so liquored up they sold out at a loss, but Fargo had warned them Austin would try to get them to sell at a lowball price. He doubted the men would be too much the worse off for it. Many of the miners had blown into Nugget with hardly more than the clothing on their backs. If they left town with two nickels rubbing together in their pockets, they were both wiser and richer for the experience.

It was almost three in the morning when Harry Austin slipped into his store and came out a few minutes later, staggering under the weight of a large bag Fargo knew was laden with gold—gold he had given the miners to flash in front of Austin to lure him into buying back their claims.

Fargo hefted a pair of binoculars he had picked up in Denver and hastily got to the roof of the bakery directly across the street from Austin's bank. The businessman looked around nervously as he lugged the gold to the front doors, fumbled with his key, and finally got inside with his treasure. Fargo watched Austin through binoculars and saw the man heave a sigh of relief at having transferred the gold from his store to the bank successfully.

A small kerosene lamp on Austin's desk blazed brightly. Fargo squinted and let his eyes adapt to the brilliance. He peered through the field glasses and watched as Austin knelt by the safe. The small vault had been placed so no one outside could directly view the dial, but Fargo had moved the mirror on Austin's desk to give a reflected view of the safe.

Fargo muttered to himself as Austin opened the safe, memorizing the combination he watched being dialed in backward. Austin swung open the steel door and heaved his bag of gold inside the small vault. A quick spin of the dial locked the safe. Austin brushed off his hands, extinguished the lamp, and left the bank.

When Austin vanished in the direction of the Lucky Nugget, Fargo dropped to the ground, put away his binoculars, and walked across the street. He had left a burlap bag of his own in the alley beside the bank. He retrieved it, struggling as much with it as Austin had with the one laden with gold.

It took him only a few seconds to slip his Arkansas toothpick between the doorjamb and the door and jimmy the catch. Fargo dragged his sack to the bank vault, stared at the combination lock and then crouched down to open the door. He licked his lips, concentrated hard, and began spinning the dial and working on the numbers he had seen in reverse. It proved harder than he had thought, but he eventually heard the distinctive metallic click of tumblers falling free.

The safe opened.

Fargo began substituting his worthless rock for the gold in Austin's bag. All this was gold he had lent to the miners, so it was still his—and yet not his, since he had only borrowed it. He was simply retrieving it for the rightful owner, he decided.

Dross substituted for the nuggets and bags of gold dust, Fargo closed the vault door and turned the dial. He frowned, wondering if Austin set it to a particular number to see if anyone had been meddling with the safe. If the businessman had done so, Fargo was lost. He had no idea what number had been under the etched arrow on the steel door.

Fargo removed the mirror from Austin's desk, then left with his treasure. There were more miners to enlist in his scheme, and he needed this gold so they could further dazzle Harry Austin.

18

"I'm getting nervous, Skye," Susanna Grafton said. She worried at a small handkerchief, turning it over and over in her hands. "He'll find out sooner or later."

Fargo started to ask whom she meant. Zeb had been working on a daily basis down at the river, and Fargo had been leaving more and more gold for him to find. He knew Austin thought they had a small mountain of gold up on the hillside, hidden under the tarp. The only thing that would give away the scheme was Austin returning and finding that all the gold was gone. Fargo had been loaning it to other miners to trade to Austin for greenbacks and the erasure of their debts.

If Zeb found out Fargo was salting the claim to lead on Austin, all hell might break loose. If Austin discovered the sham before he made a final offer for the Grafton claim, Susanna and Zeb would end up with a mound of valueless rock to show for their effort, while all the other prospectors would have gotten out of their claims, a few even making small profits.

Fargo had no illusions about the mood Austin would be in if he found out, either.

"Zeb doesn't need to know," Fargo said, staring in the direction of the river where the young man put in long, backbreaking hours panning. Over the past couple weeks Zeb had regained his strength, but Fargo worried this was as much from an improved attitude that he was finally getting gold from the claim Ben knew was there. Take away this vindication and Zeb might collapse.

If he did break down, so be it, Fargo decided. There was too much at stake to worry about the young man's attitude. Fargo had Susanna to protect from Austin's wrath—and his own back to watch.

"Oh, Zeb will be all right when he finds out," Susanna said, confirming Fargo's opinion that she was blind to her own brother's needs. He said he wanted to get rich; it went beyond that. He was living his dead brother's dream and not his own. Take the gold away and the dream died. What Zeb would be left with worried Fargo. It might be nothing more than stark hatred, for himself and the man who had engineered the scheme.

"Austin will come with guns blazing if he thinks we've swindled him."

"We're not profiting," she said primly.

"You will. This is the only claim along the river he hasn't bought back."

"First in, last out," mused Susanna. She turned so her eyes fixed Fargo like twin beacons. "What happens when he buys the claim?"

"The trap will close," Fargo said, not telling Susanna what he thought would happen. "I've found out he has borrowed heavily from banks in Denver. There's no way he can extend his credit much more. He'll be left penniless."

"But he'll get off scot-free for all his other crimes. There's Ben and—"

Fargo held up his hand to quiet her. His sharp ears picked up the sounds of a buggy rattling and clanking along the main road. In a few minutes, the sounds grew louder and Fargo knew who their company would be. He made certain his Colt rode easy in its holster.

"Let me do the dickering," he told her. "Only when Austin mentions the price we've already agreed on should you speak up."

"I remember, Skye, really I do, but he's such an evil man." Her lips thinned to a line as she glared at Harry Austin. The businessman reined back and jumped from his buggy, striding over to them as if he owned the world.

And he almost did. Except the Grafton claim.

"Top of the morning, Miss Grafton, Fargo," he said.

He didn't bother tipping his hat in the woman's direction. Fargo took that to mean Austin thought he was holding all the aces.

"What do you want, Austin?" asked Fargo, not bothering to keep the edge from his voice.

"A business deal, nothing more, nothing less." Austin fastened his thumb in the armhole of his vest and struck his pose, as if he started a long harangue.

"We haven't got all day," Fargo said. "The gold's down at the river, begging to be pulled out. Talking to you doesn't make us any richer."

"Ah yes, richer. That's what I want to make you, Miss Grafton. Richer!"

"What do you mean, sir?"

"Why, I am here to make an offer for your claim. I realize how difficult it is getting the gold out. Your brother is working his fingers to the bone and Mr. Fargo, well, he looks like he's well occupied, too." Austin could not help sneering at Fargo. If he only knew Fargo's part in bilking him, that sneer would turn to outright anger.

"I know you've bought the claims all around, Austin," Fargo said. "This one's the best. It's not for sale."

"At any price? Wouldn't you rather live the life of ease in Denver City or even back in St. Louis? You wouldn't have to rely on beggars selling you treasure maps. You'd be rich!"

"How'd you know about that?" asked Susanna, her eyes flashing.

Austin had inadvertently confirmed what Fargo had suspected. The businessman had sent out stacks of maps to lure the gullible to Nugget.

"Why," stuttered Austin, "you must have mentioned it." He realized he had made a slip of the tongue and hurried on. "Think of having servants to do your chores. Sell your claim to me and you can have that. No more living out in the wild like some kind of animal."

"She'll have a fine house and a dozen servants if she and Zeb work this claim another year or two."

"It might peter out. I'm not denying you've found a

patch of gold, but these are fickle truths. A tease, a speck of gold, then nothing but dross."

Fargo smiled a little. This was exactly what Austin would find when he examined the sack in his bank vault. Another visit the prior night had once more emptied it of gold that Fargo had cached in the wagon he had borrowed in Denver, and all the rest had been moved from the cache higher up the slope above the Graftons' camp.

"You have plenty of equipment," Austin said, pointing to the half-assembled mining equipment Fargo had brought from Denver, "but no one to operate it. My offer stands from before, I'll give you one thousand dollars for your claim."

Fargo saw Susanna's eyes narrow in anger at this. She wasn't playing her role. He hastily cut in, "Only a thousand? That hardly removes the mortgage. That can be paid off anytime." He touched his bulging shirt pocket where a single greenback poked out, hinting at the thick wad below. "The Graftons are here to get rich. Filthy rich"

"Get rich, but without also getting filthy in the process. Two thousand dollars. And that's my final offer."

Susanna's hostility died a little and she began to play her role.

"That sounds like so much, Skye. What do you think?"

"Five thousand and not a penny less," Fargo said. It was his turn to be startled when Austin answered.

"Sold!"

"You're giving us five thousand dollars?" Susanna asked, as stunned as Fargo. They had expected a long period of dickering until they finally accepted two thousand.

"It's the least I can do, considering the troubles you and your brothers have encountered," Austin said.

"You've got the money with you?" asked Fargo, still taken aback by the size of the offer.

"In my buggy," Austin confirmed. "And I have the quitclaim deeding this over to me."

Fargo and Susanna exchanged glances. Fargo knew what Austin offered was far and away more than he had for any of the other bogus claims he had sold earlier. But Fargo could not tell Austin he was paying too much without giving away how he had duped the businessman. Before Austin learned of it, Fargo wanted the Graftons to be far away.

"I'll get my brother," Susanna said, hurrying to the river to talk with Zeb. Fargo hoped she convinced him to sell before they returned. Arguing over the price might show Austin how divided they were, and if Austin even hinted at the mountain of gold supposedly cached upslope, Zeb would balk.

Austin faced Fargo after Susanna left. The man's eyes were cold.

"You should have thrown in with me, Fargo. We could have been rich."

"Five thousand for this claim makes Zeb and Susanna rich," Fargo said.

"And you'll take her share?" Austin leered. Fargo wanted to punch in the man's face for what he implied, but he held himself in check. It only convinced Fargo how crooked Austin was.

"When do you want us off the claim?" Fargo said, looking at the half-assembled equipment.

"Right away."

"You want to buy all that?" Fargo pointed to the mining equipment. "It'll take a couple days to get it packed up, otherwise."

"Another thousand," Austin said.

"Fifteen hundred," Fargo said, knowing this was a fair price.

"Done."

Again Austin startled him by agreeing so quickly.

"We'll be out of here as soon as we get our belongings into the wagons, the teams hitched and . . . some other items moved." Fargo let his eyes drift higher on the mountain, in the direction of the cache he had lured Austin to.

"No way, Fargo. You're gone now. All this goes and nothing else."

Fargo had no chance to reply, seeing that Austin

wanted him to abandon the supposed pile of gold on the mountain. Fargo had already packed up the gold he had taken twice from Austin's bank and had it in his borrowed wagon. Leaving common rocks under the tarp would be easy, but he didn't dare let Austin know.

"My sister wants to sell," Zeb said, storming into camp. "I want to stay and get rich."

"I've made my offer," Austin said smugly.

Fargo saw how Susanna held onto her brother's arm. She might have done better to simply clobber him with a rock and forge his signature on the quitclaim if he was going to argue.

"I—I agree," Zeb said unexpectedly. "My health is fading and I can't keep up the work, no matter how much gold I'm taking out."

"Good!"

Fargo saw Zeb was not sure he had done the right thing, even if he had given Austin the only argument the man would buy. The businessman returned with the papers and a stack of greenbacks. As Zeb and Susanna went over the quitclaim, Austin paid Fargo for the mining equipment.

"The machinery's good enough to pull every speck of gold out of the river," Fargo said. And it was. But the equipment could never find gold that was not there.

"Sold!" Austin said, holding up the deed with Zeb's signature still damp at the bottom. "You're got fifteen minutes to clear out."

"Fifteen!" cried Susanna. "But we have—" She saw Fargo motion to her to go along. Austin saw it, too, and grinned in triumph.

"We leave the equipment and take our belongings. Zeb, get the oxen hitched to your wagon. I'll get the mules hitched to the other wagon."

As Fargo worked to get his bedroll and tack for the Ovaro tossed into the rear of the borrowed wagon next to the bags of real gold nuggets, the wad of bills in his shirt pocket fell out. He grabbed at them, but Austin had been watching him like a hawk and saw how a few real bills had been wrapped around cut newspaper.

"Where's your money?" asked Austin, staring at the newsprint.

"Here," Fargo said, patting the pocket where he had stuffed the money he had just taken from Austin. "See you around," he said.

Austin's mouth opened and closed in confusion. Zeb got his wagon rolling and Fargo followed, leaving Austin in the middle of a now-empty camp. The businessman watched them as they rattled off, then turned and ran up the hill to the cache of fake gold. Fargo snapped the reins and kept the wagon going, heading downhill after Zeb and Susanna. The fat would be in the fire when Austin found only worthless rocks and dirt in the cache.

They had only been on the road to Denver for fifteen minutes when disaster struck.

"Look out!" Fargo shouted, but it was too late. Zeb had driven too close to the verge and let his right wheels slip into a ditch. The wagon tipped and rolled, throwing both Zeb and Susanna out.

Fargo fastened his reins around the brake and jumped out to see if they were hurt. Susanna sat up, holding her head. Her eyes fluttered open as she brushed her hair back from a shallow scratch on her forehead. It bled profusely but was superficial.

"I'm all right, Skye," she said. "How's Zeb?"

"Embarrassed," her brother said, hobbling up. "I hurt my leg and my side's starting to bleed. I popped the gunshot wound open." A spot of red spread on his shirt.

Fargo looked over the wagon and shook his head. The axle had broken and part of the wagon bed had split.

"We didn't get far enough down the road," Fargo said, looking around to get his bearings.

"What do you mean, Fargo?"

"You and Susanna get what you want to salvage out of your wagon and into mine. I've got to—"

"You've got to do nothing but die, Fargo. You cheated me!" cried Harry Austin. Bareback astride the lathered horse that had been hitched to his buggy, the man held a six-shooter in his shaking hand. Fargo would have gone for his own Colt, figuring Austin's first shot wouldn't be accurate, but he saw Austin had not come alone. Three of his henchmen were arrayed around their leader, all with rifles and six-guns pointed in his direction.

Fargo reluctantly lifted his hands and grabbed some sky.

19

"You cheated me!" Austin repeated, his voice shrill with anger.

"As if you hadn't cheated every prospector who came to Nugget," Fargo said. "You salted the claims and made even veteran prospectors think they were hitting the mother lode. What chance did greenhorns like the Graftons have?"

"They followed their own greed. Nobody forced them to buy the treasure map from those thieves back in St. Louis," Austin said, his hand trembling in rage.

"You sent out dozens of those maps, all directing the unsuspecting buyers to Nugget," Fargo said. "What did the men selling the maps get?"

"Whatever they could. I wanted people *here,*" Austin said. "Just like I want you here so I can shoot you down like a dog!"

"At least you're dirtying your own hands and not letting Whip Ballinger and Peterson kill for you anymore!"

Fargo eyed the three men with Austin and saw they were hesitant about their leader's illegal doings. This might be the first they had heard of Ballinger's murders or Marshal Peterson's corruption. Austin's staunchest lieutenants were all in custody. Whip Ballinger was off to Kansas to get his neck stretched, and Peterson was probably shouting at the top of his lungs to convince Denver's federal marshal he had nothing to do with any crime in Nugget and that it was all Austin's doing.

None of that did any good for Fargo or the Graftons.

"What's he sayin', Mr. Austin? What's he mean you been havin' Whip and the marshal kill folks for you?"

"He wants to save his miserable life, that's all," snapped Austin. "He salted the claims to make me think they were really valuable."

"You just followed your own greed," Fargo said, throwing Austin's own words back at him. "How much did you make selling supplies for twice what they were worth and peddling worthless claims? You sharing that big profit with these men?"

Fargo tensed, ready to dive to one side. He might die, but he would get one shot at Austin.

"Mr. Austin," whined one of his men, "if what he says is true and the claims ain't worth spit, then everyone'll leave Nugget and go huntin' for gold somewhere else."

"It was a sweet scheme and you destroyed it." Austin gritted his teeth and lifted his six-gun, ready to end Fargo's life.

Fargo launched himself downhill, his hand flashing for his six-shooter. He got the Colt out of its holster and cocked the hammer as Austin's first slug ripped past him, kicking dirt into his face. Blinking hard to clear his vision but still blinded, Fargo fired. His shot went wide but it spooked Austin's horse and caused a moment of confusion among his gang. Wiping his face clean with his sleeve, Fargo again saw his target clearly.

Austin tried to control his horse but only succeeded in spooking it further by firing wildly. Fargo strained to get the man in his sights but the bucking horse prevented a clean shot.

"Let's get out of here, boys," cried the most vocal of the three henchmen. They turned and started to ride off, out of Fargo's range. But Fargo stopped in wonder when he saw the men rein in hard and throw up their hands.

"Give it up, Austin. You're finished!" Cole Robby fired a round into the air over Austin's head, but the man was still fighting to regain control of his horse. The loud report was all the horse needed to really sunfish, arching its back and throwing Austin high into the air. Fargo watched as Austin turned over and crashed to the ground. The crook's six-shooter fell from his fingers and he lay gasping for air as the horse continued to crow-hop all around him.

Fargo got to his feet and ran forward, shooing off the horse. He turned and pointed his Colt directly at Austin. Fargo's finger turned white on the trigger.

Then he relaxed and stepped back.

"Come get this snake," Fargo called to the vigilantes, glaring at Austin.

Cole rode over and pointed his rifle at Austin.

"Why let him stand trial? We can string him up on yonder oak tree. It looks to have a strong enough limb."

"No," Fargo said. "I want to watch him squirm. Get him to Denver in front of a judge and jury. When those gents hear how he was swindling prospectors, I don't think they'll be too forgiving."

"And he's responsible for so many men dying," Susanna said, coming up beside Fargo. "Will he stand trial for Ben's death?"

Fargo doubted it, but Austin was in a world of trouble. After the Graftons and all the others finished testifying, Austin would be in prison for a long time. Cole and the members of the vigilance committee with him rounded up the gang, making sure Austin was securely tied.

"You took your time getting here," Fargo said, shaking Cole's hand.

"You were supposed to be a couple miles down the road before you faked a breakdown," the vigilante said.

"What are you saying?" Susanna looked confused. "How'd you know our wagon would break down?"

"Fargo here wanted you and your brother to get past where we had an ambush set up. Then he was supposed to fake the breakdown so Austin would tip his hand. We were going to nab him and all his men without having to track them down."

"But Zeb drove off the road, and we never reached where you and the others were waiting." Susanna turned pale and swallowed hard as she realized how close she had come to getting ventilated. "We almost got ourselves . . . and you . . . killed, didn't we, Skye?"

"It worked out fine. Austin spilled the beans in front of witnesses and nobody got shot. This time."

Fargo looked at the three men who had ridden with Austin and knew they would spill everything they knew, like Peterson and everyone else who had anything to do with Harry Austin. A con man was nothing more than a ringleader, and loyalty from his followers would be harder to find than gold in Austin's claims. If the judge wanted to accommodate any more witnesses against Austin, he would have to hold the trial in the city square because the Denver courthouse would burst at the seams.

"Fargo, we out-hustled the hustler," Cole laughed, glaring at Austin. Fargo caught a chuckle and soon everyone joined it at the businessman's expense.

Austin struggled in a rage, kicking, stomping, and biting at his captors. While they may have been armed, he had caught them off guard in their laughter, and before they reacted he managed to reach inside his waistband to draw his short-barreled single-shot. He fixed it right on Susanna and then took a step toward her, reached out and grabbed her by the arm, and pulled her close to him.

"Now nobody moves or I start digging a claim inside this filly's head!" His eyes locked onto Fargo's as he sprayed foam and spittle with each word.

"Drop the gun, Austin." Fargo took a step closer. "You've only got one shot and if anything happens to Miss Grafton, I don't think I could talk the vigilante crew out of ventilating you even if I wanted to."

"You won't cheat me again, Fargo." A crazed look ran through his eyes. "I'm ruined!" he screamed. "And it's all your fault!"

Fargo stopped in his tracks and motioned for the rest of the crew to back off. Austin had nothing to live for, he was a loose cannon, completely unpredictable and incredibly dangerous. No matter how quickly he and the boys moved in on him, there was no way to make sure he didn't get a shot off first.

"If it's my fault, then let her go. You've got one shot,

take me down with it instead." Fargo knew he had to get Susanna out of harm's way no matter what.

"I don't think so, Fargo. You took everything I had, and now with every gold piece you spend, I want you to remember this here pretty face and how it's all your fault that it's rotting underground with an extra hole in it." His hands shook and his voice quivered. Fargo knew there wasn't much time left.

"If you want your stinking money so badly, here." Fargo reached into his pocket and tossed the wad of bills and newspaper into the air. Austin followed the paper with his eyes before realizing he had been duped again. Susanna took advantage of the brief distraction, slamming her heel into Austin's toe, forcing him to relinquish his grip and lower his pistol. Quickly she dove out of the way as Fargo drew lead and squeezed a round out of the Colt. Austin reacted and fired his only shot, but it was too late. A cloud of gold dust exploded from Austin's piece, only to be met by the spray of blood that escaped from the gaping hole in Austin's chest. Even at a close range, the gold dust had thrown the single-shot's aim off. The Colt, however, had hit its mark as true as can be.

In a flash Susanna was safe in his arms, both their skins speckled with a golden shine. The vigilantes were speechless, amazed at what they had just seen. After the moment passed, one by one they got to their horses and headed off. Austin's men had done no wrong, and most likely they were headed back toward Nugget to gather their things before moving on. Cole and the rest of the vigilantes were on their way to Kansas City to catch the trial.

Fargo wished them a safe, quick trip and then turned to Susanna and her brother. "Into the wagon, greenhorns," he laughed. "Denver's awaitin'!"

"You are a magician, Fargo," Clem Parson said with a chuckle. He shook his head and stared at the stack of greenbacks Fargo had laid before him. "You got top dollar and now you're tellin' me I kin fetch back all that equipment and sell it again?"

"Nugget is a ghost town now that everyone knows there's no gold there. I can't imagine anyone using the equipment, and you've got all the wagons so no one's going to cart it off to some other gold strike."

"Gold," mused Parson. "That reminds me. You owe me a bit of gold. More'n a bit, actually."

"What? Why's that?" asked Susanna Grafton, coming up to where Fargo and Parson sat on the boardwalk outside the freighter's office. "Why do you owe him any gold?"

"Where do you think I got the wagon and equipment? I borrowed it all from Clem," said Fargo.

"The gold, Fargo. Don't go tryin' to cheat me out of it. I loaned you danged near a thousand dollars in gold." Parson was clucking like a hen at the thought of getting his hoard back.

"Most of it's in the back of your wagon out back," Fargo said. "In burlap bags."

"You borrowed the gold?" Susanna's ginger eyes opened wide.

"I was a fool to let him ride off with it, but I'd promised him anythin' he wanted. He done made my company with his scoutin' and I figgered I owed him. What a fool I am!"

"You made a profit on the mining equipment," Fargo said. "I'm returning all but about a hundred dollars in gold. That got lost along the way, some of the miners kept a little more then they should've, and some got lost in all the transfers that took place. For a man as greedy as he was, Austin surely was careless handling gold dust."

"Pay up. A hundred and a half ought to cover it since greenbacks ain't worth near as much as that lovely, sparklin' gold metal." Clem Parson held out his hand, waiting for Fargo to give him his due.

"I'll have to work it out," Fargo admitted. He had about fifty dollars left after all his wheeling and dealing. "But it's worth working it off stopping a skunk like Austin and sending Ballinger to the gallows."

"Good," Parson said, rubbing his calloused hands together in glee. "I'm thinkin' on a new route up to Laramie. You can scout it in less'n a month and—"

"Nonsense," said Susanna, her mouth set in determination. "Here you are, sir. Mr. Fargo saved us from a terrible fate and is worth every cent. And more." Susanna swallowed hard and Fargo barely heard her add under her breath, "Poor Ben." Louder, Susanna said, "He got our money back, and we made a small profit."

Fargo knew it was no profit at all since she had lost her brother and gone through hell and back, thanks to Harry Austin. But there had been a few minutes along the way that were pretty good for both of them.

More than a few, Fargo had to admit.

Parson's face fell. "Reckon you don't need a job. Damn." The muleteer looked up at Susanna and said, " 'Scuse me, ma'am, but you jist done me out of the best scout in all Colorado."

"In all the West," she corrected.

"I can't accept her money, Parson," said Fargo. "Not that way. I pay my own debts, and she needs to save as much as she can." Fargo looked squarely at her and asked, "What are you going to do? Return to St. Louis?"

Susanna shook her head. "I don't know, Skye. There is nothing for us there and, in spite of everything, I've taken a liking to Denver. Everything here is so . . . so alive!"

"Even as much money as you got from Austin's not going to last long because prices here are so high," Fargo said, his mind racing. "Why don't you and Zeb get jobs here?"

"Why, I don't know what I could do. I've never held a job, and neither has Zeb, not really."

"He can drive a wagon, can't he?" asked Parson. "I need a dozen drivers for the route Fargo laid out 'tween here and Kansas City. I got freight to move in a lickety-split hurry."

"I suppose he could do that, but what would I do?" Susanna asked. She looked at Fargo and saw the expression on his face. "What are you thinking, Skye?"

"I'm thinking, Parson," Fargo said, looking at the

lovely brunette but talking to the freighter, "that you need a good office manager. You can't hardly read, and I've seen how you cipher. Without an honest manager here in Denver, letting you get out on the prairie with your damned mules, you'll be out of business in a month."

"You game, Miss Grafton?" asked Parson. "Anyone Fargo vouches for is all right in my book."

"You never had a book in your life," Fargo said.

"Be that as it may, I'm offerin' her the job. So shut yer tater trap, Fargo, and let the lady speak for herself."

"I'm sure Zeb would be willing to take the job as freighter," Susanna said, "but I don't see how I could possibly take such a position." From the way she spoke, Fargo knew what she was angling for. He cursed her experiences in Nugget. It had turned her into a woman willing to barter for everything she wanted—and one who would never stop until she got it.

"That's a shame," Fargo said. "I might scout that route Parson wants a lot faster if I was reporting back to someone as pretty as you."

"What's going on?" demanded Clem Parson. "Hell, what do I care what's goin' on as long as I got both of you workin' for me!"

"When are you going to be on the trail mapping Mr. Parson's route?" Susanna asked.

"Right away," Fargo said. "The sooner I go, the quicker I can get back."

Susanna smiled and said, "There's no need to rush out until tomorrow, is there?"

Fargo decided the next morning was good enough to hit the trail.

LOOKING FORWARD!

The following is the opening section from the next novel in the exciting *Trailsman* series from Signet:

THE TRAILSMAN #237 DAKOTA DAMNATION

The Dakota Territory, 1861—where the pursuit of gold drives men to ruin, and honor among thieves is unknown.

The big man in buckskins rode alertly, his right hand resting on the smooth butt of the Colt nestled on his right hip. His piercing lake-blue eyes constantly roved the rugged terrain seeking movement. His ears, like those of his splendid pinto stallion, were pricked to catch the slightest sounds. They were winding up a narrow valley sliced by a gurgling stream, along a rutted excuse for a road that bordered the waterway. Stands of oak, cottonwoods, and ash trees towered on either side. Wildflowers sprinkled the adjacent slopes between ranks of spruce and junipers. Songbirds warbled merrily, and in a meadow to the west mule deer grazed contentedly.

A peaceful enough scene, but Skye Fargo wasn't fooled. The newly created Dakota Territory was a hotbed of violence and bloodshed. Outlaws roamed at will with little fear of being brought to bay, not when lawmen were so few and so very far between. Grizzlies marauded in large numbers. But the greatest threat, by far, was posed by the Sioux, who claimed much of the Dakota Territory as their own and keenly resented white intrusions. Lone travelers like him were easy pickings for roving bands of young warriors eager to count coup and make a name for themselves.

In the past six months alone over a dozen known deaths had been reported. That didn't take into account another seven people who went missing with no clue to their fate. As an old-timer had commented to Fargo shortly before he left Kansas City for the frontier, "The Dakota Territory ain't no place for greenhorns."

Only a few settlements had sprung up and they were well to the southeast. Fargo had passed them days ago. So when he came across a road where there shouldn't be one he decided it was worth investigating.

The sun was at its zenith. Fargo had been in the saddle since dawn and needed to stretch his legs. The Ovaro could also use a breather. A grassy clearing seemed the ideal spot. As he reined up in the center and dismounted, a squirrel scolded him from a nearby oak.

Fargo led the stallion to the stream so it could slake its thirst. Removing his hat, he slapped dust from his buckskins, then sank onto a knee and dipped his right hand in the swiftly flowing water. Cupping some, he took a few sips, savoring the cool, refreshing taste, and was about to splash some on his forehead and neck when the stallion twisted its neck to look behind them and whinnied.

In one motion Fargo spun and dropped his wet hand toward the holstered Colt, but he was still too slow. A slender figure at the edge of the trees was already holding a rifle on him, cocked and tucked to one shoulder.

"Don't even think it, mister. I'll scatter your brains from here to Sunday."

Fargo didn't know which surprised him more, that he had been caught off guard, or that the figure, who wore a floppy hat and baggy homespun clothes, was a woman.

He couldn't see much of her face, but there was no mistaking her gender. Lustrous raven curls spilled from under the hat, and the loose folds of her shirt did little to hide her more-than-ample bosom. "There's no need for the gun," he said quietly.

"I'll be the judge of that." She advanced warily, the rifle rock-steady. Fargo guessed she was in her early to middle twenties. She had full red lips perpetually formed into a delightful pucker, an oval chin, and high cheekbones. "Hike your hands and be quick about it."

Smiling, Fargo complied. "Do you live around here?"

The young woman stopped and studied him from under her hat brim. Intense green eyes raked him from head to foot. "Aubrick or Lodestone, which?"

"How's that?" Fargo responded, unsure of what she meant.

"Are your ears plugged with wax? Are you an Aubrick man or a Lodestone man?"

"Lady, I'm just passing through. I don't have any idea what you're talking about." Fargo didn't like staring down the muzzle of her Spencer. He considered jumping her and decided against it. One twitch of her finger and the rifle would go off.

The woman glanced at the sweaty Ovaro. "So you say. But you could be lyin'. Not that it matters all that much. Ma and me are well shed of the whole rotten business. It cost us too much." Her voice was a low, throaty purr. Combined with her natural beauty, it lent her a sensual allure most any male would find captivating.

Fargo wriggled his fingers. "How about letting me lower my arms? I promise to behave myself."

"You expect me to trust a total stranger?" She chuckled. "You must take me for a yack. Keep your hands right where they are. I'll be out of your hair right quick. I thought you might be one of Benedict's men—" She stopped and tilted her head, listening.

Fargo heard it, too. The drum of hoofs approaching along the road from the north. Suddenly the young woman pivoted and bolted, flying into the vegetation like a frightened doe fleeing from a pack of wolves. Not knowing what to make of her antics, Fargo dropped his hands to his sides at the very moment four riders galloped into view, riding hellbent for leather. At sight of him they slowed and veered toward the clearing.

Fargo took an instant dislike to the quartet. All four bore the unmistakable stamp of hardcases; cold, cruel expressions, revolvers tied low, and a predatory air, like four hawks swooping in for a kill. They drew rein five yards away, fanning out as they stopped.

"Who the hell are you, mister?" demanded the tallest. For his height he had a pudgy build, with considerably more stomach than chest. A Remington was strapped to his left hip, butt-forward for a cross-draw. The rest of him wore cheap store-bought clothes, a faded cowhide vest, and scuffed boots.

"Someone who doesn't like being asked questions," Fargo replied harshly.

"Isn't that a shame," said a small bundle of muscle in a fairly new short-brimmed black hat, black jacket and pants, and a black leather gun belt studded with silver stars. He had blond hair and icy gray eyes. "We mean to ask you some whether you like it or not." Sitting straighter in the saddle, he declared, "I'm Benedict. Cass Benedict."

The name was familiar. Fargo had heard it somewhere or other in his wide-flung travels, but he couldn't say exactly where.

Benedict propped both hands on his saddle horn and leaned forward. "Aubrick or Lodestone?"

There it was again. The same strange question the woman had asked. Fargo didn't answer, and after a bit the rider on the right, a stocky gent who favored a Smith and Wesson, placed his hand on it.

"Cougar got your tongue, mister?" asked the third, teasing the butt of his Smith and Wesson while he spoke. "We don't take kindly to folks who put on airs."

"And I don't take kindly to jackasses who think they can push others around," Fargo responded. He kept a steady eye on the man's gun hand, and when it wrapped around the Smith and Wesson and started to rise, he drew his Colt in a blur, thumbing back the hammer as he leveled it. In a heartbeat the stocky gunman transformed to stone with his Smith and Wesson only halfway out of its holster. "Jerk that iron and it'll be the last mistake you ever make," Fargo vowed.